MENACE FROM THE PAST

MENACE FROM THE PAST

E. C. TUBB

WILDSIDE PRESS

CONTENTS

CHAPTER I

THE FUGITIVE

The alleys of Turgan were thin fingers of twisting darkness, writhing in an intricate pattern as they wended between the high walls of ancient houses. Old were these houses, old with the slow passage of a hundred thousand years, and they stared down at the sand-filled alleys with blank faces and the blind eyes of barred doors.

Even in daylight it was hard to find a man in the maze of the old town, at night it was impossible and Fenris was glad of it.

He tensed, crouching down beside a wall smoothed to a dull polish by the whispering sand storms of Mars, and strained his ears at a subtle sound. It came again, a soft scuff of sandled feet against the dust, the harsh sound of indrawn breath, and the faint click of metal against metal as weapons touched buckles or rasped against stone.

High above the twin moons cast a faint light, a ghostly luminescence, vague and insubstantial, like the dream-glow of the Dryland Shamans and their magic globes of a long-dead science.

Fenris grinned as he heard the slow approach of cautious men, then moved carefully towards a side passage dim and black in the thin light. Behind him a man cursed as he stumbled, the sound echoing between the high walls of the deserted alley.

"Blast him! Why can't we leave it until day? We'll never find him in this rat-trap, I'm as good as lost already."

"Shut up," snapped a cold voice. "That big mouth of yours would warn a regiment. Leave it to the drylanders, they'll be able to spot him for us."

Fenris tensed, then narrowed his eyes as he caught a glimpse of a tall, lath-thin figure limned against the darkness. Of all the people on Mars only the degenerate remnants of the nomadic tribes which had once ruled all the dry sea bottoms could track a man in the darkness of Turgan. Only they could sense the alteration in the temperature of the dust where his feet had trod. They could even scent his body moisture, and their wide ears could register the very beat of his heart. For the first time Fenris felt despair.

He fumbled in the pocket of his short jacket, finding a few loose coins and a spare clip of charges for his flare-gun. He shrugged, the gun was with its belt and holster, somewhere beneath the bright lights of the spaceport five kilometers north of the old town.

But they could still be useful.

He poised the heavy clip in one hand, listening to the soft sounds of the approaching men, then he threw it from him, threw it hard against a building looming high against the stars. It struck with a metallic click and immediately a flare-gun thundered its song of power.

Lightning blazed down the twisting alley. A stabbing shaft of released energy, energy born in the heart of exploding atoms. It roared as it streamed from the pitted orifice of the weapon, and a wide patch of stone glowed with sudden incandescence.

"You fool!" The cold voice almost trembled with anger. "You trigger-happy fool! You've ruined the scent with that shot!"

"I thought I heard him," growled a heavy voice. "I thought I heard his foot hit against the wall."

"You thought!" The cold voice was thick with contempt.

"What with? Space! Why does Earth send such morons to police Mars?"

"You calling me a moron?"

"Forget it," said the cold voice tiredly. "May as well drop the search until light. The drylanders won't be able to track him now."

Fenris grinned in the darkness as he heard the soft scuff of departing feet. He could well imagine the feelings of the cold-voiced man. To find a fugitive at night in the old town would have been worth a big promotion, and they had been closer than they knew to success.

But now he was safe.

He shivered a little, drawing his short jacket tighter around his big body against the freezing chill of the night air. Steadily he began feeling his way through the dark and deserted alleys, stumbling a little and rasping his hands on the ancient stone. He saw no one, heard no one, but he knew that hidden eyes watched his every move.

It was always so in the old town at night. The high walls hid the last secrets of Mars, sheltered the dying remains of a once-mighty race, and the few descendants of that civilisation kept themselves far from both Terrestials and Drylanders. One they scorned as primitive renegades, the other...

No man knew just how the dying few of the Elder Race regarded the invading hosts from Earth. Fenris shrugged. He knew that no one would molest him here, no one that is not of Earth. His wide mouth twisted into a grin as he remembered the patrol and the too-sudden blast of energy front the flare-gun. He hadn't realised that they wanted him so badly.

He jerked to a sudden halt, his face and chest numb from an unexpected blow. Carefully he felt at the barrier stretched across the alley before him, a delicate thing of interlaced strips of metal, thin and weak seeming, yet all his strength could not even bend one of the fragile strands. He shrugged and turned back the way he had come.

Twenty paces and again he slammed into a barrier, a barrier which had not existed minutes before. He grunted, staring through the darkness in a vain effort to see who was responsible for the barriers, but the darkness pressed around him and the night was deathly still.

His fumbling hands felt an opening at his right, the mouth of a narrow passage almost too small for his wide shoulders, and after a second hesitation he plunged down it. It led into a wider pathway and he turned right, only to stagger beneath the impact of a third barrier. He turned and tried to re-enter the passage only to find it blocked with a fine lattice of metal, shrugging, he followed the left-hand path, his feet whispering as his knee boots ploughed through the dust.

Fifty paces he took, fifty long strides, then came to where three alleys converged. Across two of them stretched the thin strands of metal barriers, the other was left clear, and for a long moment Fenris stood and stared at the dark opening in the ghost-light of the racing moons.

"Where are you?" His voice echoed from stone whispering through the darkness like the rustle of disturbed ghosts. "Show yourself!"

Silence.

"What are you doing? Where do you want me to go?" He stared at the high blank walls of the buildings, conscious of hidden eyes peering down through the misty darkness.

Still nothing.

He grunted, shifting his feet in the dust, then abruptly lunged towards one of the barriers. He sprang, his feet driving at the dust covering the alley, his big hands grasping the top of the delicate looking barrier. Muscles surged beneath his shirt and his boots rasped against the interlaced strands as he pulled himself up and almost over the barrier.

Almost.

Fire seared through him. A wash of stabbing energy twisting nerves and muscles, blasting at sinew and tendon, bringing quick sweat to his face and neck with the unexpected pain.

He dropped, writhing on the sand, his body a tormented mass of quivering flesh and bone. Cramp seized him, doubling him up in savage agony, and making him roll in the dust with mind-searing torment. It passed, and slowly he regained his feet, standing on quivering legs.

"I understand," he said bitterly to the darkness and the silence.

"You want me to go somewhere, all right then, I'll go, but where?"

A faint wind blew down the alleys, sending little ripples over the fine dust, scraping tiny particle against tiny particle with a thin whisper of sound, a ghost murmur, as of thin voices long dead and almost forgotten.

Fenris shivered, his skin crawling to the bite of the cold night air, then plunged down the single unbarred opening. He walked carefully, keeping to the centre of the dust-filled alley, his hand brushing against one wall, his eyes wide and strained as they peered into the darkness.

Other barriers loomed before him, forcing him to turn and weave between the high walls of the enigmatic buildings, and always he was conscious of watching eyes. Alien, unfathomable, strangely disturbing eyes. The eyes of a race that should have been long dead.

How long he walked he never knew. He had lost all track of time, but the racing moons had dropped below the tops of the high buildings, and the stars burned in the deep velvet of the sky with all their naked brilliance.

His lungs ached with the constant effort necessary to oxygenate his blood, and the chill of the freezing night had numbed hands and feet, arms and legs, back and shoulders.

He was staggering when he slammed into another barrier.

He grinned weakly as he clutched it. It barred his path with its delicate metallic strands, and it crossed a passage down which there had been no openings, no cross paths, and somehow he knew that he had reached the end of his nightmare journey.

For a long time he sagged against the barrier, his mouth open as he sucked air, fighting a battle with the insidious effects of too much exertion in too thin an atmosphere. He shook his head driving some of the dimness from his vision, then for the first time saw the door.

It lay to his right, one of the sunken doors of old Turgan, but this one was different, this one had a thread of light spilling from its edges.

He grinned as he pushed it open.

CHAPTER II

REFUGE FOR THE HUNTED

Inside it was warm and bright and noisy, noisy with the cheerful sounds of many men, a noise which stopped with sudden abruptness as he staggered into the brightly lit room.

He swayed a little, sucking at the rich air gushing from an oxygen regenerator, and the gas cleared the numbness from his mind and body. He grinned down at the men sitting around a long table of ancient wood, hard faced men, men from the cess pools of space, men with watchful eyes and weapon-loaded belts, ready to kill or be killed at a wrong word or a wrong gesture.

"Who are you?"

A man at the head of the table snapped the question. A big man, no longer young but with a barrel chest and thick limbs betraying mighty strength. A mane of red hair hung almost down to his eyes and one cheek and ear had been scarred with a flare-gun blast, the wound long healed now and puckering his harsh mouth into a deceptive grin.

Fenris nodded towards him, and eagerly gulped at a container of thin purple wine.

"Just a stranger," he said coolly. "Just passing through you might say." He stared at the big man. "I don't ask questions and I don't answer them. I don't see what I'm not supposed to see, and I don't want to be seen. Good enough?"

"No!" The scarred man leapt to his feet, his harsh mouth twisting in sudden rage. "That's not good enough, nowhere near good enough." He glared at the young man. "My name's Branson, Captain Branson, maybe you've heard of me?"

"Maybe."

"Then you'll know better than to step on the wrong toes. Now. Who are you?"

"I told you once," said Fenris calmly. "A stranger. Let's leave it at that shall we?"

For a moment he thought that the Captain would spring at him, and he tensed, poising on the balls of his feet, the big container of wine ready in his hand. Then Branson snorted, and a thin-faced man sitting beside him touched his arm, speaking rapidly in a low voice. Branson nodded, and the thin-faced man looked at Fenris.

"How did you get here?"

"Walked."

"I know that, but how did you find this room?"

Fenris looked at him, then at the circle of watching men, then at the big Captain. They all seemed to have the same expression, a tense expression as if the answer to that question was of supreme importance. He shrugged.

"I was invited," he said carefully. "At least you could call it that, I had no choice but to come here."

"The barriers?" snapped the thin-faced man.

Fenris nodded.

"I knew it." He stared triumphantly at the big Captain. "My name is Setter, the Captain you know, and you'll find out about the rest of us later." The thin-faced man gestured towards the watching men and they relaxed, their hands drifting away from their holstered weapons. "Now, friend. What's your name?"

"Does it matter?" Fenris stared at Setter and grinned. "After tonight I doubt if we'll ever see each other again, and anyway, what's in a name?"

"Nothing. You the man the patrol was hunting for?"

"Maybe."

Setter grinned, showing his teeth in a wolfish snarl, and the big Captain grunted something beneath his breath.

"Look, friend," said Setter patiently. "I can appreciate a man who likes to keep things to himself, but this is one time when that isn't possible. You've got nothing to be afraid of, every man here is in the same position as you are. We ducked into the old town to escape the patrol—and we couldn't get out! We arrived at this room the same way as you did, and we're all in this together. Now relax and have a bite of food and drink and talk a while."

He grinned his wolfish smile again and thrust a lump of synthetic bread and a thermocan of vitaminised soup across the table. Fenris took them, thumbing in the top of the cone shaped can, and swirling it between his palms while he waited for the built in chemical unit to heat the liquid.

"I'm Fenris," he said abruptly. "Had a little trouble with a man at the edge of the spaceport. He set the patrol on my tail and I had to duck into Turgan to throw them off. The rest I suppose you know."

"What sort of trouble, Fenris?" Setter stared across the table, the single portable glow tube reflected from his eyes. "Murder?"

"No. I'd taken a ship into a repair yard for overhaul. I was low on cash and he gave me a good price for the entire job so I left it with him and worked at the field for a while."

"Filling pits?"

"Yes." The young man stared at Setter. You know about it?"

"No."

Fenris shrugged.

"You know the routine, a ship lands, the jets fuse the sand and blasts a pit on the field. We had to fill in, they gave me a small tractor-dozer for the job and I made out well enough, living in the barracks and eating at the mess."

"Then what?"

"I went back to the yard for my ship. The man had done the job—so he said, but when I was just past Deimos I found out just what he'd done."

Fenris paused, little spots of colour flaming high on both cheeks.

"The louse had botched the job! He'd used inferior materials and used fleximetal instead of welds. Luckily I had to apply max stress to dodge a meteor, and the Bernheart just collapsed beneath the strain. I had to call a tug to get me back to Marsport."

Branson said something and reached for the container of purple wine, and from the assembled men came a low animal-like growling. What the repair man had done was the worst possible crime. Too many men had died in space, too many men had gasped out their lives in the tiny confines of a ship because of botched jobs and cheating repair work. Out in space the chances of being picked up were small, and many crimes had been hidden merely because those who could complain were dead and drifting in the void.

"The tug cost me all I could raise from selling the ship, and the law suits to recover my money and claim damages would have cost even more than that." Fenris rubbed his knuckles, a tight smile of his wide mouth.

"So I came back to Turgan, and had an interview with the man. He didn't seem to want to give me back my money. I gathered that he has the local police pretty much under his thumb, and they leave him alone while he pays off to their welfare funds."

Anger darkened the young man's features.

"The swine! Selling men for the sake of graft! No wonder rats like that can get away with murder!"

"What did you do?" Setter licked his thin lips and the men hunched closer to the table. Fenris grinned.

"I beat him up," he said softly. "I used my flare-gun to smash his face in, and then I used it to wreck his repair yard. I must have blasted a fuel store, he must have been crazy to have stored fuel there anyway, and the whole thing went up in a cloud of smoke and flame. He'll do no more botched jobs on space ships, he'll ruin no more Bernheart engines."

Fenris sipped at his steaming soup and looked at the assembled men.

"The rest you can guess. The patrol chased me and I had to dive into the old town to escape. They had drylanders with them and once they almost had me. After that I wandered about a little, then barriers began shooting up all round me electrified at that, one of them almost killed me."

He winced at the recollection of the punishing current.

"I've never heard of them before," he said thoughtfully. "Somehow, for some reason, the Martians drove me here like a stray dog, drove me here to this room. Why?"

Setter shrugged.

"That's what we all want to know," he said in his dry voice. "I've been here two weeks now, and some of the others have been here longer than that."

"Then why not leave?"

"How? The barriers are there at night, and the patrols watch by day." The thin-faced man grinned as he gestured towards the table. "Anyway why should we leave? Here there is food, drink, a measure of comfort, while outside?" He shrugged and made a wry expression'. "Better to let the heat die off anyway," he said, and the men muttered their agreement.

Looking at them Fenris could tell why. It was a safe gamble to bet that everyone in the room was wanted by the police for some reason or other. Aside from himself and the two at the head of the table, five other fugitives rested their arms on the ancient wood and stared dully at the brilliance of the portable glow tube. For the most part they looked what they were, the scum of space, but one lad seemed different and watching him. Fenris could tell why.

He had the space-light in his eyes. The heart-stopping hunger of the very young, the lust for adventure and the craving for the new and exciting. Fenris stared at him, remembering his own youth, the days when he had watched the ships of space lift from the landing fields and dart into the great Unknown. He had felt that hunger, and before he'd reached maturity had trod the alien soil of a dozen worlds and Asteroids. Now...?

He sighed, remembering the too-swift disillusionment, the hard earned knowledge, the collapsing of bright dreams and brighter hope. He was still young, not more than thirty, but watching the lad made him feel very old. The youngster felt eyes upon him and raised his head.

"Hello." Fenris grinned and thrust the jug of wine across the table. "What's your name?"

"Jarl."

"Pretty young aren't you?"

"What's it to you?"

"Nothing." Fenris still smiled but when he spoke his voice had a bite as of frozen steel. "We could be friends," he suggested, "or if you prefer it that way, we could be enemies. What's it to be?"

"Just leave me alone can't you?"

"Sure, but sometimes a man needs a friend. Especially when he's a long way from home and the cards seem to run against him." He grinned at the youngster's too-bright eyes and slapped him on the shoulder. "How old are you, son?"

"Eighteen."

"A nice age. The age when a man could get married to some nice girl and make a place for himself somewhere. You got a girl?"

"No."

"A home? Folks of your own?"

"No."

"Been travelling long?"

"Long enough."

Fenris sighed and took a deep drink of the thin purple wine. For some reason he seemed strangely drawn to the youngster, perhaps because he seemed so young and helpless, or perhaps it was because Fenris remembered his own youth too vividly. It hadn't been an easy time. He had slaved on the Asteroids, hauling fragments of a long-disrupted planet to the smelters am depots, fighting off claim jumpers and risking his life every moment of the day.

He'd done a spell on Mercury, servicing the big solar power plants there, struggling in a suit three times heavier than he was and feeling the savage bite of radiation burns searing his skin. He'd known what it was to be stranded on Venus, where a man paid as he ate, or he didn't eat. He'd worked in a dive on Io, helping to rob spacemen at rigged card games and selling cut liquor to alcohol starved natives. He'd served time on the Moon, and served time on Mars. He'd stowed away on a ship, then watched while most of the crew died of plague and the Captain went insane.

He'd done most things, and done them the hard way, and their trace was written plain on the wide planes of his features and the scars on his big, well-muscled body.

He looked up at the sudden opening of the door, then stared, the container of wine falling from his hand to spill on the floor.

Something entered the room.

CHAPTER III

THE GORGON

It was tall, incredibly tall, and robed in a thick material of deep and sombre brown. Two things which could have been arms stirred beneath the robe and something blurred and white showed dimly beneath the hooded cowl. Staring at it Fenris felt a quick curiosity, then the figure moved a little, the cowl gaping and the white blur beneath it coming into sharper focus.

Suddenly Fenris lost his curiosity.

He didn't want to see what was hidden beneath the robe. He didn't want any part of it. Like most spacemen he had heard rumours, tales whispered over the drink-stained tables of a thousand taverns on a handful of planets, and like most men had nodded and secretly doubted their grain of truth, but he doubted no longer.

The thing beneath the robe wasn't human!

It rippled with a peculiar serpentine grace, seeming to glide across the floor and around it hung a faint odour, the musty, acrid odour of life that had been hatched rather than born. It glided into a corner, and around the table the men sat as though carved from stone.

For a long moment nothing happened, then Branson snarled a curse and reared from the table, a flare-gun heavy in his hand.

"Who are you? What are you doing here?" His face reddened as he spat the questions, and the heavy pistol trembled in his hand.

Setter clutched at the big Captain's arm, his thin lips whispering quick words as he forced the big man back into his chair.

The alien didn't stir, didn't move, and watching the cowled and robed figure, Fenris had the peculiar conviction that it was...

Waiting!

Waiting for something to happen, or for someone to come. Perhaps waiting for someone to do something, say something, even to suggest something. The feeling grew almost overpowering as they sat there, the men at the table and the strange figure almost invisible in the dim shadows of a corner.

Jarl whimpered, his wide eyes scared and glistening with fear. Setter licked his thin lips, his mouth twisted in its wolfish grin. Branson sat, the pistol forgotten in his hand, and great beads of sweat starting from his florid features.

Fenris sucked a great lungful of air, his hand closing around the smooth neck of a container of wine, his muscles tensing for the throw. He couldn't help it. Every primitive instinct within him shrieked for him to destroy the thing standing in the corner.

It was a blind reaction to the unknown, a hidden response born of the old days when primitive man fought for possession of his world.

Fenris was spaceman enough not to be shocked by other-world beings, he had seen the crystalline inhabitants of Mercury, the leathery creatures of Jupiter's Satellites, the strange mutating life of Venus' swamplands. He had spoken to great insects, eaten with things sprouting tendrils and crawling on their multiple feet, but this was something different.

This was danger!

He rose from the table, the muscles of shoulder and back, of hand and arm, tense and quivering as he raised the container of wine. His arm jerked, started forward—and a pale ray of peculiar blue luminescence darted from somewhere beneath the robe.

It fanned out as it left the silent shape in the shadow filled corner. It hummed a little as it clove the air, singing a thin high note of quivering vibration. It struck full against the hand and arm of the young man, and suddenly, it was as if they had turned to stone.

The container of wine fell from a nerveless hand, crashing to the table and sending a shower of purple over the ancient wood. Fenris stared at his hand as it followed the path of the jug. It thudded against the table, but he felt nothing, as if his hand were severed from his body, or as if it belonged to someone else. He stared at it, at the numb heaviness of his arm, and he knew that if the pale blue ray had struck his body he would be dead, his heart stopped, his brain frozen, his lungs paralysed in his chest.

Slowly, terribly slowly, with lancing fingers of fire and nerve-wrenching agony, life returned to the paralysed hand and arm. He stood waiting for the effect of the ray to die, biting his lips against the pain, his eyes twin pools of torment against the sudden pallor of his face.

"Kill it," a voice whispered and with a shock he recognised it for his own. "Kill the damn thing. Now!"

No one moved. No one reached for a gun to blast the stranger standing silently in the corner. No one did anything except stare with sick and horrified eyes.

Still the tension increased, mounting with a mind-shattering effect of overstrained nerves and subtle waves of hidden emotion. Fenris wiped blood from his bitten lips, and knew that unless something happened the limit of tolerance would be reached and the man would break into berserker rage or quivering impotence. Somehow he didn't think it would be rage.

A shadow moved outside the open door. A drifting something, veiled, slender, walking on two legs and with two arms. Silently the newcomer crossed the room and stood beside the alien shape. Silently it raised its hands and slipped back the cowl of midnight silk, and Fenris heard the gasp of utter amazement from the tense throats of eight men.

The newcomer was a girl!

She was young, fantastically young, with a wealth of dark hair and a soft bloom on her cheeks that spoke of perfect health. She opened her eyes, and they were twin pools of clearest blue. She smiled, and her scarlet lips parted to reveal shining white teeth. She spoke, and her voice was soft and gentle as the ripple of a Terrestial brook on a summer's day.

"I am the voice," she said. "I will explain."

"What!" Fenris lunged forward, his eyes cold against the harshness of his features. "What do you mean?"

"Through me will you learn of what is to be done, what must be done, and why." She paused and the cowled figure at her side seemed to sway a little towards her as if whispering quick words.

"First. I am of Earth, not of Mars. My parents died in a rocket crash and I was flung from the burning wreck to die upon the sands. That was a long time ago, and since then I have lived with the..." She frowned, as if finding it difficult to translate a word into Terran.

"With those?" Fenris pointed towards the silent figure standing in the corner. "You mean that those things took care of you, brought you up, taught you?"

"Yes."

"Incredible!" He slumped down into a chair his eyes thoughtful as he stared at the fresh young features of the girl. "Yet I suppose it could happen, but why? Why?"

"It was necessary," she said calmly. "I shall explain."

"Then explain," he snapped. "What is this all about? Why are we here? What is that thing in the corner? Talk, and talk fast!"

"First. You are here for a purpose. You are men hunted by the peoples of your own race, desperate men, men who have nothing to lose and all to gain. You were 'collected' guided or driven to this room where you have waited to learn the reason for your being. If you wish you are free to leave, but I must warn you the police of your race are waiting outside the area of old Turgan."

"I'm not leaving," said Setter. "They want me bad and I don't reckon on serving life on Jupiter. I wouldn't last a year under that gravity."

"I'm staying," echoed Branson. He didn't explain why. The rest of them muttered their desire to remain, and Fenris grinned as the girl stared at him.

"I'll stay," he said grimly. "I don't like it out. I'll stay. I like the prospect of filling blast pits for the next ten years even less than what's in this room."

She nodded, not surprised, and Fenris wondered again at her intimacy with the strangely cowled creature standing silently in the shadowed corner.

"Now. You must know that what lies before you is no easy thing. There are dangers, great dangers but the rewards will be high and you will have ample protection."

"You speak of dangers," said Fenris slowly. "In what form will this danger appear?"

"That I cannot tell you, but no journey is without its dangers."

"A journey?" He looked sharply at her. "To where?"

"To another place."

"A planet? An Asteroid? Where?"

"To none of those. To another dimension, another vibration level. Can you understand the concept?"

"Yes, but can you?" He stared at her, and read his answer in the blankness of her eyes. "Tell me, do you speak for yourself or for the creature standing beside you?"

"For..." She hesitated, her face twisting with something like pain, and she swayed a little, placing her hand against her temple. She straightened, and when she spoke her voice was somehow cold and utterly inhuman.

"It is necessary that I speak through this, our instrument," she said, and Fenris knew that the words originated from the cowled thing standing in the shadowed corner.

"I must be brief and you must understand without question. It is necessary for us, the small remnant of my race to make a journey. We will provide the vessel and you will act as crew. You are men without hope, but we can offer you much wealth and you will be safe as long as you do as we command."

"To where?"

"To another universe, a different vibratory plane of co-existence, to a similar world to the one on which we now stand. It has taken many millennia to build the vessel, repair it rather for none in this solar system has the technology necessary to build such a craft. For reasons not essential for you to know, we are unable to operate the ship, we need men, such men as yourselves, and to this end we saved the life of this woman so that she could act as an instrument between us."

"That was good of you," said Fenris sarcastically. "You seem to expect us to take a lot on trust. How do we know that you won't just shoot us when we've done your dirty work? Or turn us over to the patrols?"

"You don't," said the alien voice calmly. "But rid your minds of such petty thoughts. We have greater things than to betray those who help us."

"Fair enough, you could probably do it anyway." Fenris rubbed his arm as he remembered the effect of the strange blue ray. "Who are you anyway? Martians?"

"No, we are not of this world."

"From Earth then?"

"Yes."

"You mean that you originated on Earth?"

"No. We came to Mars from Earth. We arrived on Earth from our own world, our own level of vibration."

"I see." Fenris narrowed his eyes in sudden thought. "That ray! The one that paralysed my arm!"

"Yes?"

"The Gorgons! They were supposed to turn people into stone and that ray would certainly have that effect. To a primitive people a paralysis beam such as that would form the basis of a legend! You did come to Earth and in a way you still live there in myth."

"It is possible. I seem to remember the incident, a race of separate tribes of no technical advancement. As I remember it became necessary to protect our vessel from their barbarous attack."

"Is that why you left Earth?"

"No. The gravity of that planet was far too high for our comfort. We came here, and the natives of this place have served as our hosts for many millennia."

"I see, and now you want to get back home." Fenris nodded.

It sounded reasonable, very reasonable, and somehow the prospect of such an adventure appealed to him. He stared around the table, and saw that the other men felt the same way.

"You agree to operate our vessel then?" The inhuman voice seemed tired as if the strange creature found the task of controlling the vocal cords of the girl too much for its strength.

"Yes." Fenris looked at the assembled men. "How about you?"

They nodded their assent, their eyes glowing with the prospect of adventure and easy wealth and the young man grinned as he saw their tell-tale expressions. They were scum, these men, driftwood of the vast sea of space, and yet the very thing that had made them what they were fitted them for the proposer adventure. Restless men, money-hungry men, in another age they would have been pirates, mercenaries, pioneers, straining at new frontiers or grabbing for a comfortable life.

"That is well. At the next time of darkness you will be taken to the ship. In the meantime rest, for there is still much for you to do."

The girl sagged, her young features suddenly drawn and tired. She smiled at them, a hesitant smile and Fenris smiled a little as he saw how her eyes rested on the fresh face of Jarl. The youngster flushed and stared at his hands.

"Tell me," said Fenris abruptly. "Are you coming on the trip?"

"But naturally, how else would the..." Again she frowned and the young man supplied the missing word.

"Gorgons," he said, and she nodded after a moment's thought.

"Gorgons, a good a name as any. Well then, how else would the Gorgons communicate with you?"

"Can't they write?"

"Write?"

"Draw marks on a piece of paper," snapped Fenris impatiently. "Or don't you know what writing is?"

"I have never heard of it, the Gorgons use electrical recordings for the storing of knowledge, recordings which are attuned directly to the brain."

He shrugged and watched the two strangely dissimilar figures as they drifted on soundless feet from the room. The door swung softly shut behind them, and Fenris drew a deep breath of relief. He was annoyed and surprised to find his hands trembling, and his face was damp with sweat.

Quickly he reached for the wine.

CHAPTER IV

MARTIAN GUIDE

The night wore on and day threw its harsh light over the horizon. The stars dimmed in the sky, but still glowed like dim ghosts across the dark blue, almost black, bowl of the heavens.

Fenris sighed, lifting his head from where it had rested on his folded arms, and rubbed thoughtfully at the stubble coating his lips and chin.

The others were still asleep, the big Captain snoring, his mouth open and his florid features twitching to some vague dream. Fenris grinned and rose softly from the table.

Branson wore two guns, two heavy flare-pistols in separate holsters belted around his sagging paunch. Carefully the young men unstrapped one of the guns, slipping the belt from around the sleeping man and buckling it around his own slender waist. Carefully he checked the weapon, examining the swollen bulk of the firing chamber, slipping the fully charged clip from the butt and squinting at the pitted orifice.

He poised the heavy weapon in his hand, then slipped it back into its holster, adjusting the leather to a comfortable position. Then he tried the door, and finding it open, emerged into the maze of alleys of old Turgan.

The barrier was gone.

The alleys stretched before him, dust filled and silent in the early morning light. To either side the blank walls of high buildings reared upwards, and their barred doors made a row of indentations in the polished stone.

A faint humming drifted from the sky, and Fenris crouched within a doorway, his eyes hard as they stared at the strip of sky between the, buildings.

A machine droned over the city, a thing of bright metal and plastic, with the shimmering wheel of rotating vanes glistening above it, and the faint trails of jet exhausts showing white against the dark blue sky.

A patrol ship!

He grinned as he watched it quartering the city, and he could imagine the sharp eyes peering down from the hover-plane, radioing instructions to the ground patrols searching the town. He waited until the machine had droned past and then returned to the room, locking the door carefully behind him, and grinning at the startled expressions on the faces of the waking men.

"It told the truth," he said calmly. "The barriers are gone but the town is thick with police. They've even got the hover-planes out and if we left this room we wouldn't stand a chance."

"I could have told you that," yawned Setter. He narrowed his eyes at the sight of the weapon around the young man's waist, and his own hands darted to his belt. "Where did you get that gun?"

"Found it," said Fenris calmly. He grinned at the florid face of the big captain. "I borrowed it from you, Branson. No man wants two flare-guns, if he can't hit his target with one then two are just extra weight to haul around. Any objections?"

"Why you..." The big man jerked to his feet and the movement of his hand was deceptively fast. He clawed at the weapon in his belt, then his hand froze as he stared down the pitted orifice of a heavy flare-gun.

"Take it easy," warned Fenris quietly. "You had two guns and I had none. If you want it that much you can try and take it back, but you'll have to do it the hard way, Branson." He grinned, the flare-gun poised easily in his hand. "Do you still want it back?"

"You stole it," snarled the big man. "Took it while I was asleep."

"Would you have given it to me?" Fenris shrugged slipped the weapon back into its holster. "Look," he said quietly. "We've all agreed to stick together, to form a crew to operate that alien's ship. We don't know where we're going or what we'll find when we get there. One thing is certain, it isn't going to be a picnic, and the quicker we realise that the better."

He stared at the wakeful men.

"Now. I suggest that we form a crew, weld ourselves into close-knit unit, that way we'll be better prepared to defend ourselves. Even if the alien ship doesn't operate, still we stand better chance of escaping from this trap as a unit than as collection of individuals. What do you say?"

"He's right," said Setter, his thin lips twisting into a wolf-snarl. "Relax, Branson, you can always get another gun but you can't always get a man to use it."

"How about it, Branson? You willing to let me keep the gun?"

The big Captain nodded, the scar tissue on his cheek livid against the stubble surrounding it.

"Yes, but don't try anything like that again, Fenris, you won't get away with it twice."

"Good enough." The young man shrugged carelessly and grinned at the strained face of the youngster. He winked and Jarl grinned and winked back.

"Now. Who's going to be the Boss?"

They stared at each other, the men watching both the big Captain and the whipcord body of the young man. Setter licked his thin lips and jerked his head towards Branson.

"I vote for him. He's had the experience."

"I say we follow Fenris," said Jarl in his young voice, then stared down at his hands as the men looked at him.

"I agree with Setter," said Fenris surprisingly and nodded towards the scarred Captain. "I've heard of you, Branson. You took a crippled ship through the Asteroid Belt one time didn't you? Piloting by luck and instinct, and with the patrol ships hard on your tail. You're the man who run the Venusian Blockade that time during the Three Years War, and escaped by circling the Sun within three million miles from the corona."

"He's the man," said Setter, and the big Captain grinned.

"Then he's the man we need to lead us." Fenris stared at the watchful men. "I can handle a ship and I can repair an engine. I can plot a course and fire a turret gun with the best of them, but Branson has something I haven't got. Experience. The knowledge that can only be won the hard way, by living long enough to learn by actually doing. I vote for Branson as Captain."

They nodded at that, their hard eyes gleaming in their hard faces.

"I vote Fenris for Mate." Setter looked down the table. "I'll act as Bos'n, the lad as steward, and the rest of you as gunners, engineers, look-outs, anything that has to be done. Agreed?"

"Agreed," said Fenris, and the rest of them muttered their acceptance of the plan.

"One more thing," said the young man. "The girl will be coming with us, you all know why, but I want to warn you now. She is not to be touched. If any of you get bright ideas about her then he'll have to deal with me, and I promise you, I'll burn him down like a dog. That girl is our only contact with the Gorgons, and if we upset her, then we may upset them, and that's something I don't want to do—yet."

"You got ideas, Fenris?" Branson wrinkled his scarred cheek as he stared at his Mate. "You think that we can't trust them?"

"I don't know," said the young man slowly. "Maybe it's just me, but I don't like them, I feel something wrong somewhere."

He shrugged and gave a short laugh. "Forget it, we can take care of ourselves if we have to."

"I didn't like that thing either," said the big Captain slowly. "It reminded me of something I met once, a thing on Ganymede, a thing that looked like a stone but wasn't. I'd sat down beside it, not knowing what it was, and I remember that I felt just the same as I did last night. I felt uncomfortable, tensed... afraid I guess, but I was stubborn and so didn't move."

"What happened?"

"It almost got me," said the big man simply. "It split and before I could move it had stuck half a dozen hollow spines into me and was sucking my blood. I was lucky, I had a flare-gun in my hand, and I managed to blast it before I lost too much blood." He shuddered at the memory. "I've never liked Ganymede since."

Fenris nodded, then stiffened, his hand flashing towards his holstered weapon as a thin grating noise came from the back of the room, and a pivoted stone swung slowly open.

Cold blew through the opening, a dry biting chill and with it came a musty odour, a smell of dust and age and things long dead. Light glowed through the opening, and a shadow loomed large against the hidden source of the glow.

Fenris gulped, then thrust the flare-gun back into its holster, staring at the half-mythical figure of a Martian of the ancient city of Turgan.

It was tall, and by Terrestrial standards, painfully thin. It had huge soft eyes and the white skin was covered with a short and delicate fur. A long robe hid most of the body and

Fenris knew that the chest would be huge and the limbs frail, a result of the lesser gravitation. A naked skull showed above the robe and eight-fingered hands showed pale against the dark material of the robe. A thin, lipless mouth parted revealing toothless gums, and when the Martian spoke its voice was as the dry rustle of long-dead leaves.

"You will follow me," it whispered. "The Old Ones have sent me to be your guide."

"The Old Ones?" Fenris stepped forward and stared at the Martian. "The Gorgons? The thing which was here last night?"

"Yes."

"I see." Suspicion narrowed the young man's eyes, and he murmured softly in the difficult tongue of dying Mars.

"You do not like these people," he said gently. "For how long have they rested on the necks of your race?"

"Too long," replied the Martian in the same language, and his eyes widened in surprise as he stared at Fenris. "You speak our tongue; that is strange, not many of Earth trouble to learn the ways of Mars."

"I did," said the young adventurer softly. "I have troubled to learn many things, and I have respected what I have learned. Tell me, do you help the Gorgons from love or from fear?"

"From fear."

"I guessed as much, we of Earth and Mars are too close for either of us to welcome such things as those. Now I understand why you trapped the Terrestrials, hid them in your city, you are eager for the Gorgons to be gone."

"That is so."

"Why?"

Fenris snapped the word, his eyes glittering as he stared at the impassive features of the old Martian. "What is it that you know and will not tell?"

"There are things of which I may not speak, but this I can tell you. For several millennia now the beings which you call

'Gorgons' have resided here with us. They have taken the produce of our dying race, used the few hours we each can spare from the necessity of servicing our machines, and their weight has been a great burden."

"They will be gone soon," urged Fenris swiftly. "Soon they will be unable to do you harm. Anything that you tell me now may be of great importance later on. Why do you dislike them so?"

The Martian remained silent, staring with great eyes at the tense face of the young adventurer, and Fenris sighed. He knew of the ancient ways of the Martians, sometimes they would speak and at others not. No man knew just what moves guided them, or which customs governed their way of life. The two races remained apart save for an occasional mingling when the professors and scientists tried to salvage something of the long dead science which had built the mighty canals, but aside from that Earthmen and Martian remained strictly apart.

"I give you thanks," he murmured in the whispering syllables of the ancient language. "May your path be damp with soft rains."

"May your path be dewed with plentiful moisture," replied the Martian politely, and gestured towards the opening behind him.

"Will it please you to follow me?"

"We will follow," promised Fenris, and gestured towards the watching men. They thrust forward and together Fenris and the old Martian stepped into the secret passage.

Behind them the great stone swung silently back into the solid wall.

CHAPTER V

THE SHIP OF THE GORGONS

The way was long and little plumes of dust rose from beneath their feet, filling the thin air with a dusty fog, and making their eyes burn from contact with the tiny particles. The Martian led the way, his oddly fashioned lamp throwing distorted shadows on the smooth stone of the walls, and steadily they moved ever downwards, away from the sun and air, the bleak plains of the old sea bottoms, marching downwards to dim and secret caverns.

They walked for a long time. They walked until their feet dragged in the dust and their faces were stained a dirty brown with the pluming sand. Fenris walked just behind the Martian, and his hand ached from its grip on the worn butt of his gun.

"How much further?" He spoke in the old tongue and the Martian answered without halting or turning his head.

"A little way now, a few steps more."

Fenris grunted, stumbled on the uneven sand, then stopped, his eyes widening at what they saw.

A cavern loomed before them. A titanic hollow beneath the crust of Mars, a huge place, its vastness lost in shadows and seeming to be filled with tiny points of flickering luminescence.

It stretched before them, the narrow walls of the passage widening and losing themselves in distance. The roof was beyond sight and the floor was covered with the eternal red dust of Mars. Light from the oddly fashioned lantern held by the old Martian sprayed on the machine-cut walls, lit with a dim suspicion of a glow the beginnings of an arching roof, and touched their faces with its harsh white brilliance.

In the centre of the cavern rested a ship.

It was such a vessel as none of them had ever seen before. A thing of distorted planes and eye-wrenching curves, of twisted angles and strange construction. It was made of some black material, dull and seeming to absorb the light of the blazing lantern, sombre and somehow vaguely menacing.

It squatted on the fine red dust like a thing from some tormented nightmare, like an alien creation fashioned after laws unknown to normal space and time.

The ship of the Gorgons!

Lights flickered around it, the brilliant points of light cast from portable lanterns, and Martians worked around the ship, their wide eyes dull with some nameless emotion and their thin bodies sagging with utter weariness. They worked with a strange desperation these remnants of a race which had been old when man had first dropped from the safety of his trees. They worked with oddly shaped tools and strange pieces of metal, and the noise of their labour echoed throughout the cavern with as thin whispering, as of atoms crying out in their tiny voices of pain.

Fenris stared, then took a step forward, his eyes hard and cold as he watched the sagging bodies of the weak Martians as they laboured over the alien vessel.

"Why don't they take a rest?" His voice slashed through the darkness and echoed from the distant walls. "Why don't they call a halt? Look at them, they're almost dropping on their feet."

"It is well to speed the departing guest," whispered their guide, and had he been an Earthman his voice might have held irony. "We are happy to see them go."

"But you don't have to kill yourselves doing it." Fenris shook his head and turned to the big Captain at his side. "That's the ship, Branson. Think you can handle it?"

The big man shrugged, his florid features pale in the light from the lantern, the scar tissue on his cheek puckering his lips into its eternal grin.

"If it can respond to control, move and lift off the planet, then I can handle it." He squinted at the ebon ship. "But how does it operate? Where are the venturis? The landing fins, the loading ports, the atmosphere controls?" He bit his lip as he stared at the vessel, then shrugged. "I'll handle it, somehow."

Fenris grunted, then strode across the dry sand towards the waiting ship, the others straggling in a loose group behind him. He walked almost up to the strange ebon metal of the vessel, then blinked as his eyes tried to follow the twisting lines of the plates and vanes. He felt a sudden nausea, a sickening vertigo, and closed his eyes against the alien convulsions of lines and curves. He staggered a little, resting his hand against the side of the ship to recover his balance, then snatched it away with a cry of pain.

It was cold. Cold with the utter absence of heat, of energy, of molecular motion. It was so cold that his breath froze on the metal, then fell away in a tiny cloud of snow, and the flesh of his hand where he had rested it on the metal was raw and bleeding with the loss of a section of skin.

"Watch it!" He snapped the warning at a man who seemed about to touch the ship. "That's not normal metal, it'll take the skin off your hand if you touch it as it did mine." He frowned as pain lanced from his injured hand, then wrapped a handkerchief over the wound.

"I should have warned you," said the Martian regretfully. "Many of my people have suffered grave wounds from merely touching the vessel, we had great trouble in repairing a rent in the hull."

"You would have," said Fenris grimly. He narrowed his eyes as he stared at the ship. "The metal must be a perfect medium for absorbing energy," he mused. "Light, heat, even cosmic rays and free radiation must be soaked up by it. Perhaps they have some form of converting plant for changing the absorbed energy into usable power."

He turned as footsteps rustled across the sand.

The girl stood before him and with her, like an attendant shadow, the oddly disturbing figure of the cowled alien. Fenris grinned at her, and gestured towards the strange vessel.

"Well," he said tightly. "Are you ready to give us our first lesson?"

"Yes," she said, and from her lips spilled the rapid syllables of old Martian as she rapped orders to their guide.

"Your work has finished. Depart with your people. You know what must still be done."

"I hear and obey," he whispered, and Fenris cringed to hear the subservience in his tone. The Martian bowed, not towards the girl but towards the silent figure hidden in its cowl, then he turned and the light from his lantern faded into the distance as he walked across the muffling sand.

After him went the crowd of weary workers, their eyes dull with utter fatigue and their lights bobbing like distant stars as they wended their way across the cavern floor. After a long moment there was silence, and darkness, and utter cold.

"Shall we begin?" Fenris forced himself to speak quietly though his nerves crawled beneath his skin and his hand ached as it gripped the butt of his flare-gun.

"We begin."

Light glowed with abrupt suddenness from the metal of the ship. A scintillating glow of dancing atoms, as if some of the energy absorbed by the alien metal were being released in a stream of flickering particles of pure light. It grew, and in the glow the faces of the men looked pale and strained as they hunched close together for mutual comfort.

The voice of the girl echoed with a strange eeriness in the silence of the cavern and Fenris knew that it was the alien, and not the girl, who spoke.

"The outer hull is composed of a substance which has the power to absorb and transmit all kinds of radiant energy. This energy can be converted to usable power and so the vessel can replenish its power supplies from any convenient source of radiant energy, a sun, a world of heat, even the offensive weapons of your race, and so it also serves as an excellent protection. Normally, even though there is always some free energy in space, the use of power is greater than the replenishment, and so it is necessary to recharge the accumulators before starting on our flight. This we will do from the solar furnace."

"The Sun!" A man gulped and looked at Fenris with something like horror. Like all spacemen he had a healthy respect for the sun and knew what could happen if a ship drove too close to the thin line between danger and safety. The tremendous gravitational drag of the sun made it impossible for a ship to pull free once it had ventured too close, and the terrible heat would melt the toughest steel, roasting the crew and exploding the fuel.

"The drive is not as your reaction tubes," droned the cold voice. "The ship is moved by an alteration in space-time reference planes, an involved system of sub-spatial tensors which resolve on pure mathematics, which I doubt whether you will be able to understand,"

"Then how can we operate the ship?"

"A control cabin similar to the one used on your primitive space ships has been installed, also one of your Bernheart engines for reaction drive. We have coupled the controls together so that while you will appear to use familiar controls, yet the ship will respond to our own mechanisms."

"Logical, but one more thing." Fenris stared coldly at the cowled figure standing beside the girl. "Why do you need us to operate the ship at all? Why not just pilot it yourself?"

"We are no longer able to do that," said the alien, and the droning voice seemed oddly menacing. "For long ages we have lived here beneath the surface of this planet, and we have lost much of our strength. It is for that reason that we are returning to our own universe, yours lacks a subtle radiation essential to our well-being. We are no longer capable of the normal stress of space flight, and so we have employed you to act as our crew. During the trip we will rest in tanks of nutrient fluid."

"I see." Fenris shrugged. "Your reasons can remain your own as long as we are well paid for what we do."

He grinned at the strained features of the big Captain.

"Branson. Better come aboard and take command. The quicker we get out of here the better I shall like it."

"I know how you feel," grunted the big man. He stepped forward and stared at the glowing metal of the ship. "How do we get inside?"

With startling abruptness a hole yawned in the side of the metal. It opened as the iris shutter of a camera opens, widening from the centre out, and, after a moment's hesitation, Branson stepped into the brightly lit interior of the ship.

Fenris followed him then Setter, then Jarl, and the rest of the crew. The girl came after and the robed figure of the alien last. It stared at the opening, and with the same abruptness with which it had opened, it closed, leaving a smooth expanse of unmarked metal.

"Neat," said Fenris drily. "What now?"

"The control room." The girl led the way towards a section of the vessel and the men followed her, trying not to look at the eye-twisting curves of walls and bulkheads within the ship.

"This is where you will operate the ship." The girl pointed towards a door, and opening it, they found themselves in the counterpart of a standard control room. "And here is where you will rest when not on duty." A second door gave onto a small room containing bunks and stacked with cases of thermocans and water.

"On no account will you leave this section of the vessel," she ordered. "The trip should not take long and you have plenty of food and water for your needs. One other thing."

"Yes?" Fenris glared at the cowled figure of the alien, feeling his nerves tense again as they had in the room, wanting to draw his flare-gun and blast the alien to greasy ash.

"This." She pointed towards a small tube. A seat was mounted behind it, and it faced a blank wall of metal. "If we are attacked you must press this button here, the wall will become transparent and you must aim the small tube on the attacking vessel. When you have centred it press this second button. That is all."

"If you say so," said Fenris dubiously, "but I'd rather sit in a turret and operate a heavy duty flare-cannon. Are you sur that thing will work?"

"It will work," she promised, then staggered a little as she had done once before. Fenris caught her in his arms and forced her into a chair.

"Steady," he said gently. "Are you better now?"

"Yes. Yes thank you." She struggled to rise but he held her down and she relaxed against the cushioned softness.

"What's your name?"

"Name?" She frowned. "What do you mean?"

"What do they call you? Surely you know what a name is?" Fenris frowned down at her, then smiled at her puzzled expression.

"Never mind, I'll give you one." He thought for a moment. "Lorna. How about Lorna? Do you like that?"

"Lorna," she repeated slowly, then smiled. "Lorna."

That's right. Now my name is Fenris. The big man is called Branson and the one with the wolf-grin is Setter. This youngster here is Jarl." He jerked his head at the lad. "Jarl. Come over and meet Lorna."

Jarl flushed, biting his lips and clenching his hands. He seemed very young, far too young for the heavy weapon belted around his slim waist and the surface air of cynical knowledge which he normally affected.

"I want you to take care of her, lad," said Fenris quietly. "Teach her all you know and get to know her as well as you can."

"Sure, Fenris, but why?"

"Don't question your luck, son," grinned the tall adventurer. He narrowed his eyes as he stared around the control room. "The Gorgon? Where is it?"

"Must have ducked back into the ship," snapped Branson from where he sat studying the controls. "I tried to follow him but the door's locked and we can't get out."

"Can't we?" Fenris sprang to the door barring the control room and living quarters from the rest of the ship, then stiffened as words began pouring from between the lips of the whitefaced girl.

"Take your stations. We leave immediately."

"Leave?" Branson stared at the girl then at his visi-screen. "What does it mean, 'leave'? I can't blast through solid rock!"

"Do not question," snapped the coldly alien voice from the girl. "Merely do as I order."

For a long moment silence hung thickly on the air, then... "Take off! Now!"

Branson stared at the wall of rock before and above. He looked at Fenris, then at the girl, and shrugged.

Slowly he moved the levers that would send them crashing against the solid walls of the cavern.

CHAPTER VI

BATTLE IN SPACE

The ship jerked, tilted, seemed to rise from the sand and hurl itself towards the roof of the huge cavern. Branson stared at the visi-screens, great beads of sweat starting out on his florid face and his hands trembling as they rested on the controls.

"Cut the drive!" Setter grabbed at the big Captain's arm, then reeled back with a snarl as Fenris pulled him away.

"Leave it alone." He grinned at the little man and nodded towards the rear of the ship. "They know what they're doing. Don't forget, they are on this ship too and they love their lives as much as we do. Just relax, we won't crash."

"But the cavern! Man we'll smash against solid stone!" The little man almost gibbered in fear and rage, then fell silent, watching the flaring visi-screens and the swift approach of the smoothed rock.

It rushed at them, limned in the infra-red heat register of the visi-screens, hard and bleak, bearing the unmistakable signs of having been gouged out of solid stone by a race now long dead. It filled the screen, almost it seemed the strange hull of the ship touched it, then…

Light blazed around them, the dying light of the setting sun, the wan light of the racing moons and the ghost glitter of the distant stars.

"We're through!" Setter gibbered his amazement as he stared at the visi-screens. "We passed through solid rock!"

"Remember what the Gorgon told us?" Fenris twisted his lips in a tight smile as he glanced at the little man. "This vessel does not use normal methods of propulsion. He said that it moves by a constantly shifting space-time reference, I don't know what he meant, but it's obvious that the ship must move in a series of jerks. One second we were within the cavern, the next we are here. Somehow we just didn't pass through the space between them, somehow we must have passed around that space."

"I don't get it," grumbled the big Captain. He squinted at the graduations on the visi-screen and adjusted his controls. "What made the ship take a jump at the exact moment we were about to crash?"

"I don't know," admitted the tall adventurer. "Perhaps it wasn't that at all, but something else." He frowned in deep thought for a moment, then snapped his fingers.

"Got it! Remember how the metal of the hull absorbed all energy? Well. When we hit the cavern roof what happened?"

"You mean what should have happened." Branson glared at the controls, then slowly nodded. "I get it. Normally we would have smashed into the rock and heat would have resulted from kinetic energy. You mean that the hull absorbed all that energy and so let us pass through?"

"What else? The hull couldn't be damaged. Before that could happen the rock had to touch it, touch it with crushing force. Naturally the rock couldn't do that, we were the ones moving, not the cavern. As the rock tried to absorb the energy of our momentum it heated, the hull soaked up the released energy, and in effect we bored a hole straight through the roof of the cavern."

He stared down at the dwindling city of old Turgan, at the eternal sand of the dry sea bottoms, and at the bright lights of the new town to the north.

"Naturally we can't do that to any great mass. I doubt whether we could absorb the energy of a fairly large meteor for example, but the roof must have been fairly thin, and so we just dived straight through."

Branson grunted, busy with his controls. Beneath his hands the ship quivered with strident life, the plates of the alien hull seeming to moan a low dirge as they shot up through the thin atmosphere of Mars.

"We need more power," said the big Captain. He jerked his thumb towards what seemed to be a regular fuel gauge. Its thin hand hovered low on the scale, very nearly touching the red danger area, and Fenris stared thoughtfully at the other instruments.

"They certainly fitted this ship up," he mused. "It must have taken quite a while, and how did they know just what the normal control panel would look like?"

Branson shrugged, his eyes flickering over the gauges before him.

"I don't know, but if that thing was right we'd better head straight for the sun and recharge the accumulators."

He swore as a light flashed red on the panel before him, and a sharp hum sounded warningly together with the light. Setter spun the visi-screen controls, and as he adjusted the magnification, two bright flecks glowed on the screen. They expanded, swelling and growing as they came nearer, and Fenris thinned his lips as he recognised them for what they were.

"Patrol ships! Two of them and headed this way."

"Can you shake them?" Setter leaned across the instrument board and clutched at Branson's arm. "Captain! Can you get away?"

"I don't know." Grimly the big Captain slid levers down their grooves, and watched with strained eyes as the two advancing ships began to fall behind. For a moment it seemed they would outrun the patrol ships, then Setter groaned and Branson breathed a curse.

"They've got auxiliaries, booster rockets to step up their acceleration, we don't stand a chance."

"Can you dodge them?" Fenris stared at the visi-screen, his eyes cold as he saw the gun-loaded turrets and the snouting menace of multiple cannon.

"Daren't chance it. If that gauge reads true we need every erg of energy we carry to get into an orbit around the sun." Branson slumped at his controls and shook his head. "Nothing more we can do. This crate doesn't seem to have the driving power of straight jets." He snarled a curse as he slammed his big fist down onto the padded arm of his chair. "What the devil did they fit Bernheart's for if they didn't intend to use them? Now all we can do is wait until those ships decide to blast us to dust."

"Will they do that?" Setter stared at the Captain then at the figure of the tall adventurer. "Won't they give us a chance to surrender?"

"They're probably doing that right now," said Fenris grimly. "We haven't got a radio and we can't put out signal lights. We are in an alien ship of an unfamiliar pattern and we don't answer their signals. What else can they do but blast us?"

He frowned, then his eyes brightened as he stared at the little tubes and their mounted seats.

"Look! Remember what the girl told us? If we were to be attacked use these things." Swiftly he slipped into one of the seats, the little man settling himself into the other. Deliberately they pressed the first buttons and Fenris heard the Bosun gasp as the metal wall before them turned transparent and as clear as glass.

"We'll wait until they actually fire," snapped Fenris. "Maybe we can cripple them a little with these things, slow them down and give ourselves a chance to escape."

He gripped the base of the tube and on the transparent wall before him, a tiny spot of brilliant light moved in tune to the motion of the tube. Fenris stared at it, then grinned as he recognised the sighting device. Tensely he waited as the two patrol ships came nearer, their rocket exhausts streaming behind them and their gun turrets swinging a little as they tracked the alien vessel.

"How do you operate this thing?" Setter mumbled as he swung the tube, and Fenris snapped quick instructions to the little man as he watched the advancing ships of the Martian Patrol.

"Aim with that spot of light. When you've centred it, press the button at the base of the tube. Aim for their jets, we may be able to cripple them, let them drift until they can be picked up by a tug."

From the nose of one of the vessels a streamer of flame lanced into the void. It lengthened, widening as it came, and at its tip rode a lambent ball of searing energy. It spat towards them, before them, and exploded in a soundless flare of brilliance well ahead of their nose.

"Warning shot," gritted Fenris. He tightened his hands on the little tube, straining to keep the tiny point of light centred on the spouting rocket tubes of the patrol vessel. "The next one should hit smack in our belly."

"Like hell it will!" Setter crouched over the little tube and Fenris could see the sweat glistening on the little man's face and neck. "When do we fire these things?"

Again the patrol ships fired their forward cannon. Flame lashed from the speeding vessels, widening and spreading across the void in an eye-searing pattern of atomic brilliance. Again the shots missed, but this time they were closer, much closer, and Branson muttered from his seat at the controls.

"Almost within effective area. Better try and stop them, Fenris."

"Right." Fenris stared at the little man. "Ready, Setter? Aim for their jets. Now!"

Deliberately he pressed the button at the base of the tube, the tiny point of light aimed directly on the swollen venturis of the advancing ship. Something streamed from somewhere outside the alien ship. A pale ray of writhing green light, twisting and jerking as it hurled across the void towards the flaring jets of the patrol craft. It struck, seemed to flow with a peculiar hungry motion, and then...

The ship had vanished!

Fenris stared at the transparent wall before him, his eyes still aching from having tried to follow the writhing thread of green. He blinked, stared, then slowly pressed the button returning the wall to its normal opaqueness.

"Did you stop them?" Branson looked up from his instruments, his florid features tense with strain. "We soaked up some energy from their shots but used it and more when you fired those tubes. What happened?"

"They vanished," said Fenris slowly. He stared at the little man. "Setter. Did your ship vanish too?"

"Yes. Went out like a light when the green ray hit." The little man licked nervously at his thin lips. "Maybe my aim wasn't too straight, I was scared of missing so I may have aimed a little too far forwards, but the ship vanished just the same."

"I don't think it mattered where the shots hit." Fenris strode across the cluttered control room and stared into the visi-screens. They were dark, space was empty of any mass of any importance. "That green ray must have set off a chain reaction, a consuming fire which burned the ships as if they had been moths in a flame. The crews didn't stand a chance."

For a long moment they stood there, the men impressed to operate the alien vessel, and their faces were pale as they realised just what power they had at their command. Setter licked his lips and stared at the big Captain. Fenris watched him, then stared at the others, and they all had the same expression. Even Jarl had it, and somehow Fenris knew that he wore it himself.

"Gets you doesn't it?" He jerked his head towards the little tubes, pitiful looking, seeming to be no more than a couple of flashlights. "With a ship like this and weapons like those the system could be ours. We wouldn't have to worry about fuel, just drop into an orbit around the sun. No patrol ship could take us, we could blast them to dust with those gadgets there. With this ship we could pirate every cargo in space. Is that what you're thinking?"

They didn't answer, but he read his reply on their faces.

"I don't blame you. I've thought of it too, but where would it get us? Money, a few years of luxury, then the hunt would catch up with us and we'd end in the flame-chair or be thrown to the void, alive, in a space suit, and with ten hours air. Which would you choose?"

"They've got to catch us first," snarled Setter. The little man twitched his head towards the rear of the vessel. "They promised us payment didn't they? Well, I say we ask for this ship. Agreed?"

"Yes," said Fenris quietly. "We will demand this ship, but not to go pirating with. No. We'll take it to Earth, let the scientists look over it, solve what makes it work, and then we'll sell the secrets and live rich and honest for the rest of our long, long lives."

He grinned as he saw their expressions alter, the atmosphere of strain die and vanish in a roar of good humoured laughter. Even Setter grinned, his thin lips writhing in their wolf-smile, and Branson chuckled from his seat at the controls.

"Good for you, Fenris. I've seen too many fools grab at the obvious and miss the main chance. This ship is worth more to us as an honest possession than we could ever get robbing the space lanes."

"Yes," said Fenris quietly. "I lost a good friend that way, he made a grab at a load of irillium in transit on a mail rocket. They caught him of course, you can't dispose of irillium without too many questions being asked. They caught him because he didn't have money to buy a passage from the Asteroids, no money, and he carried a fortune in his pocket. They caught him and he gasped his life out somewhere in space, locked in a suit with his ten hours air, and heading somewhere towards Altair."

He paused, looking at their strained faces, then smiled at Jarl and crossed the room to stand before the girl.

"Better get some rest, Lorna," he said gently. "Jarl. Find her a room somewhere where she can be alone."

"That is not necessary," she said softly. "I have quarters next to the section of the ship where the Gorgons live. They arranged matters so, for it will be essential for me at times to contact them, for you will require fresh instructions after we have charged the vessel."

"I see. Then get to them, we will be approaching the sun soon and that will not be pleasant." He smiled down at her, then jerked his head at the youngsters and watched them move down the corridor.

Setter stared at him, then glanced at the watching men.

"How near to the sun must we go?" His voice shook a little and Fenris could sense his fear.

"That depends on the Captain," he said calmly. "Better get to your bunk now, and the rest of you also. Get some rest, we may need every scrap of strength later on, and there may not be time for sleeping."

He waited until they had filed into the living quarters, then crossed the control room and stared at the smooth surface of the visi-screens.

"How long?" He glanced at the tense face of the big Captain as he adjusted the controls, familiarizing himself with their feel. Branson shrugged.

"I don't know, but it shouldn't be long; this ship is fast."

"What orbit will you take? Fontieuls?"

"Maybe. Fontieuls orbit requires too much delicate handling and one slip could mean the end. The best I can do is to swing in a closed circle, how near we can get depends on the way I can handle this ship."

"Having trouble with it?"

"Trouble!" Branson slammed his hand down on the arm of his padded chair. "I don't know the thrust. I don't know the mass, the acceleration, the velocity, the heat index or the fusing point of the outer hull. I have no idea what the fuel consumption rate will be and I don't know what the storage is. Everything I should know I have to guess at and you ask if there's trouble!"

Fenris grinned and slapped the big man on the shoulder.

"You'll get us through," he said with quiet confidence. "That's why you're the Captain."

Before them the ball of the sun glowed with incandescent glory.

CHAPTER VII

THE MAN WITHOUT BONES

The Sun!

A tremendous ball of atomic flame, searing, scintillating with the Phoenix Reaction, the building up of helium from hydrogen and the smashing of the heavier elements back to the primeval ones. Energy was released on that cycle, torrents of energy, light and heat and the entire range of the wave-spectrum. It had gone on for millions of years and would go on for millions more. It would last until the great orb of the sun collapsed in on itself, the lighter elements of its construction converted to the dense, terribly heavy neutronium, and then it would be a white dwarf, small and white and cold, its radiation trapped by its own gravitational field.

But now it was flaming in all its stupendous glory.

Fenris stared at it, his eyes narrowed against the glare, and felt his skin cringe with the instinctive reflex action of any spaceman when too near the solar furnace. They had passed the misty ball of Venus, the half-molten, half-frozen orb of Mercury; and now they swung within five million miles of the great ball of atomic reaction.

And Branson was worried.

He spoke his fears to Fenris as he sweated over the unfamiliar controls, keeping his voice low so that the other shouldn't hear, and his hands trembled a little as he adjusted the levers, adjusted, constantly adjusting the one thing which stood between them and utter destruction.

"I don't like this, Fenris, I don't like it at all. The hull is absorbing energy too slowly, the accumulators are barely charging as it is, our drain is too great."

"Maybe there's a critical period. Maybe they will charge faster later on."

"Maybe, but what's going to happen to us if they don't?" Branson wiped sweat from his florid features and glared at the young man. "Damn those slimy things back there! How in hell's name can I operate this ship without information? For all I know a connection has broken, a plate fused, anything. We might be plunging to our death this very minute, and I wouldn't know a thing about it until it's too late."

"I know, but what can we do?" Fenris bit his lip and stared at the flaring surface of the mighty sun. He squinted at it, then turned the light-transmission index of the visi-screens down even lower than what it was.

"We must get nearer," he said quietly. "As it is we are using almost as much energy as we absorb in keeping this orbit. If we venture closer we can charge the accumulators faster and use less energy."

"Closer!" Branson stared at the tall adventurer and shook his head. "Are you insane? With a strange ship and no energy? How can we get closer without burning up?"

"You're forgetting the hull." Fenris twisted his lips in a tight grin. "This isn't a normal ship remember. We won't fuse the hull as we would on a regular craft, it will soak up the heat and radiation, convert it into energy, the very energy we must have. I tell you, Branson we've no choice. You've got to take us nearer to the surface!"

"No!"

"You must! We can't swing around and around like this. If the heat doesn't kill us, and thanks to the hull there's no danger of that, what of the radiation? Maybe the hull is transforming it and charging the accumulators, but maybe it isn't.

Perhaps we are all dying of gamma rays this very moment, or some other radiation may be affecting our cells. You've got to get in closer!"

"I can't do that, Fenris. I daren't!"

"Why not? You've been closer than this before. In an ordinary ship with an ordinary hull. Three million miles wasn't it? Three million and with this ship you could do even better than that."

"No, Fenris. No." Branson's florid features paled as he gripped the controls. "You don't know what it was like then. You can't know. The heat, the radiation, we were almost roasting I tell you. No. I won't do it again, not for you and certainly not for those slimy things crouching back there in their damn tanks. No!"

"Why not?" Fenris stooped low over the big Captain. "Forget the heat, it won't worry us. The radiation we must chance, we can't do anything about that. There's only one thing left, the gravitational drag. Can you calculate the speed necessary to swing us into a closed orbit say within three million?"

"Are you crazy? We'd never manage a closed orbit within three million miles. We just couldn't make the speed, and if we did we'd tend to be thrown out of orbit all the time. We can't do it that way I tell you."

"Then which way can we do it?"

"Use a parabolic sweep. We'll fling the ship in a closed orbit all right, but it will be in the form of an ellipse. One focal point will be the sun and the other will be twenty million miles out. We'll dive towards the sun, build up speed, as much speed as this crate will stand, then swing close and let the gravity pull snatch us round in a closed curve. That's the way I did it before and that's the only way possible to do it at all."

Fenris grinned as he saw the big Captain adjust his controls. What he had said was correct. They couldn't continue orbiting the sun for an indefinite period, if for no other reason than that of the Solar Patrol. The tremendously powerful ships of the patrol would certainly spot them, and he knew that he could never again use the alien weapon against men again.

It was too much like murder.

Setter glared at him as he entered the living quarters and he sat beside the man, reaching for a thermocan of vitamin-ised soup and thrusting in the top with a practised movement of his thumb "Something on your mind, Setter?"

"Yes. When are we going to start the journey?"

Fenris took a long drink of the steaming soup and carefully set down the half-empty can.

"You mean when do we start the trans-dimensional shift?" Fenris shrugged. "Just as soon as we recharge the accumulators. Why?"

"I don't like this," muttered the little man. "A straight journey I don't mind, I'd ride a rocket to Pluto or to Hell, it's all the same to me, but I don't like playing games with the Sun."

"I know how you feel," said the tall adventurer. He reached for the thermocan and drained it of the hot soup. "Unfortunately there's nothing else we can do. We've got to charge the accumulators, we can't break away if we don't much less start the journey, and so you've just got to stand it for a while." He frowned as he stared around the room, counting the men lying half-asleep in their bunks or sitting at the table drinking their soup.

"Setter. We're one short? A thick-set man, Hammond I think his name was. Where is he?"

"Hammond?" The little man glanced around the room, the shrugged. "Maybe he went exploring. Maybe he's crept in corner somewhere. What's the difference?"

"Perhaps you're right," said Fenris carelessly. "He can't get off the ship that's certain and we can find him when we want him." He slammed down the empty container and rose to his feet. "I'll get back to the control room, Branson may need some help; you follow after you've had your meal." He grinned down at the worried face of the little man, and moved with long strides towards the control room, his skin prickling with an irritating itching.

Branson glanced up from where he crouched over the controls and Fenris slipped into the co-pilot's chair at his side.

"How's it going, Captain?"

"Bad." The big man jerked his head towards the visi-screens. "I'm taking a chance, letting us fall directly towards the sun and trusting that whatever drive this thing has can pull us out of it." His lips tightened over his teeth as he adjusted the controls, and Fenris leaned forward, his eyes narrowed as he stared at the seething hell below.

It boiled like the surface of a storm-lashed ocean, a sea of flame torn and wrenched by internal stress and the twisting effects of the huge sunspots darkening the luminescent surface. Titanic fingers of flame leapt from that surface, huge masses of incandescent gas, leaping thousands of miles from the glowing sun and hesitating for a, long minute before sinking down to rejoin the turbulent sea.

Again the prominences sprang high into space thrust from the central mass by some strange reversal of gravitation, then glowed with hungry fires as they sank back to the mighty core of the solar furnace.

The black maws of sunspots gaped like ugly sores against the brightness, the flocculi twisting and writhing with startling brightness at their edges. Others opened, dark against the eye-searing brightness of the surrounding gaseous envelope, exposing for a moment the innermost depths of the titanic atomic furnace.

Fenris shuddered and glanced towards the fuel gauge.

The thin hand had crept up from the red danger area and was now almost a quarter of the way across the dial. The hull was absorbing and transforming the colossal energy of the sun into usable power, but slowly, too slowly, and he tensed as Branson muttered something between a curse and a prayer.

"This is it, Fenris. If this crate can't move fast enough we'll all go to flaming ruin!"

Tensely they watched as the surface below seemed to leap at them with the promise of horrible death. They were falling towards it, would fall into it, dragged by the awful power of the tremendous gravity unless...

Unless they could gain enough speed so that the ship could extend the curve, could move fast enough so that instead of falling directly into the sun they could swing into an orbit around it, letting the gravitational field drag them in a circle instead of pulling them straight down.

For a long while they stared at the glowing surface streaking below. Branson sat like a man of stone, his big hands tense on the controls, the sweat trickling from his face and the scar tissue on his cheek livid against his pallor. Fenris sat and waited, waited as thin hands moved across graduated dials, as the transmitted image of the sun showing in the visi-screens swelled a little, then steadied, then incredibly seemed to shrink.

He gasped, and the pain in his chest told him that he had held his breath too long, the quivering of his hands that he had sat tense and strained for an unremembered period of time.

"Made it!"

Branson sagged, deep lines of weariness tracing their path from nose and eyes. He wiped sweat from his face and neck, then lurched to his feet.

"Watch it, Fenris. The controls are set, the route is now automatic, we are in an orbit around the sun and we can stay there until the accumulators are fully charged."

"I'll watch it," promised the tall adventurer. "You go and get some food and rest. I'll call you when the gauge reads full, though breaking from the orbit should be simple enough."

"Yes?" Branson paused, his hand resting on the back of his padded chair. "Just how would you do it? Blast straight away?"

"No. Just increase speed in the direction of travel. As our speed increases so would the orbit widen until we could snap away from it and head for outer space." He grinned at the big man and glanced at the visi-screens. "Go and eat now, I'll take care of this, and if you see Jarl tell him I want him."

"Sure." Branson staggered a little as he crossed the room. "Maybe you should have been the Captain."

"No. Any fool knows how to break out of an orbit, but it takes more than just brains to get into one, it takes experience. You're the right man for the job, Captain, and don't forget it."

He turned back to the screens as the big man staggered from the control room, and watched the incandescent surface of the sun as it swept below. In the screens the great ball seemed like a curved plain of heaving gas, a plain rimmed with a faint haze, the haze of the corona, that halo which could be seen flaring out for thousands of miles whenever the central ball was occluded by an eclipse.

Something flashed on the edge of the screen something bright and moving with terrific velocity, huge and somehow alien to the natural fury of the Sun. It streaked across the viewplate of the screen, glittering like a miniature sun, and Fenris stared at it, recognising it for what it was.

A ship of the Solar Patrol.

A huge vessel, powered with the force of exploding atoms, armoured with layer after layer of radiation resistant metal, the outer hull polished to mirror brightness to reflect as much of the heat as possible. It swam in the upper layers of the gaseous envelope, in a tight orbit and in eternal free fall. Men rode within the ship, some of the toughest men to be found in the entire System, and they watched and registered, observed and correlated, probing the mighty furnace to learn the hidden secrets of the Phoenix Reaction.

One day they would find it. One day they would discover the hidden secrets locked in the heart of that raging furnace, and when they did, then men would head for the stars.

Watching them made Fenris proud to be a man.

He could guess what it was like within the heat-blistered hulls of the Sun Ships. The air would be burning hot, the water would boil and the very metal of the inner hull would be too hot to touch. Even with full refrigeration, with the best insulation known to science, with multiple hulls and polished surfaces, yet the terrible energy streaming from the sun would make life a living hell.

He thinned his lips as he watched the burning brightness of the Sun Ship as it swept across the visi-screens. They needed the metal of which the alien ship was made, the energy absorbing metal of the outer hull, and the secrets of transforming that raw energy into usable power. With such a secret men could learn the mysterious powers of the solar furnace, and with those powers, could build the starships which would give mankind a universe to roam in instead of a handful of planets.

Fenris grinned a little, a tight grin, and one without humour.

He would get that secret for them. He would bring back this ship for the scientists to examine, to tear apart and rebuild for human hands to operate, and if for no other reason, he would be glad when the journey was over.

He looked up from the visi-screens as Setter entered the control room. The little man seemed worried and he chewed nervously at his lips, his thin mouth twisted in a half-snarl, half-grin, as he stared at the tall adventurer.

"I can't find Hammond," he said abruptly. "I've looked everywhere for him, and he's not in this section of the ship at all."

"That's impossible!" Fenris glanced at the instrument panel and rose to his feet. "He couldn't have vanished, the ship is sealed and he couldn't have jumped into space. He must be here."

"Well he isn't." Setter glanced nervously over his shoulder and lowered his voice. "He isn't in this section of the ship," he repeated, "but what about the other part?"

"Where the Gorgons are?" Fenris nodded. "But how could he get in there? I thought that section was sealed."

"So it is, but one of the men said that he saw Hammond staring at the wall. It's just possible he managed to find a way in I'm worried, Fenris, there's something going on which I don't like."

He stiffened, his thin features white and ghastly beneath the cold light of the glow-tubes, and Fenris felt his nerves quiver to the impact of a shocking sound.

A scream echoed through the ship.

A man's scream, a yell of horror, of fear, of sickening terror. It bounced from the walls and bulkheads, trembled in the air vibrated from the very controls themselves.

Before it had died away Fenris was racing towards the living quarters, Setter close at his heels. In the big room a thing staggered about in the centre of the floor.

It was a man, but now it looked less like a man than a thing from a twisted nightmare. It moved with little jerking motions, and its eyes were pits of blankness in the bone-whiteness of it face. It sagged in a revolting way, and even as they watched, the legs folded, the arms hung limp, and with a peculiar soggy sound it collapsed to the metal of the floor.

It rippled, a strange movement of muscle and tendon, of sinew and cell. It seemed to shrink, to fall inwards on itself, and suddenly Fenris felt very sick.

"It's got no bones," he whispered. "The skeleton has gone, look at that face! Look at that face!"

Silence hung like a shroud over the horrified men.

CHAPTER VIII

JOURNEY TO ANOTHER UNIVERSE

Fenris stood in the centre of the room and his cold eyes flickered from one to the other of the watching men. He frowned, staring down at the crumpled thing at his feet, and fought the rising tide of nausea churning his stomach.

"What is it?" Setter gulped as he wiped sweat from his face and neck. "What is that thing?"

"That was Hammond," said Fenris quietly. He stooped over the crumpled heap and forced himself to examine the flaccid ruin of what had once been a man. Carefully he touched the paper-white skin, lifted one limp arm, and letting it fall with a soggy thud to the metal of the floor. He rose, and his face was tense and strained, his eyes like chips of frozen steel, and when he spoke his voice was like the rasping of files on adamantine steel.

"What did this? What strange energy has done this to a man?"

"What has happened to him?" Branson leaned forward as he stared at the thing on the floor. Fenris stared at the big Captain, then at the thin faced little man, finally at the rest of the crew.

"Something has dissolved the bones in Hammond's body," he said tightly. "He was dying when he came in here, his limbs unable to support his weight, his skull collapsing on his brain, his chest caving inwards on his lungs and heart. Look at him! A bag of skin filled with flesh and blood, but no bone, not a single vestige of bone. Something has dissolved them and I want to know what that something is!"

Silence returned, weighted with menace and unspoken horror. A man licked his lips and cleared his throat with a nervous sound.

"I think that he went back there." He jerked his head towards the rear of the ship, the section holding the mysterious Gorgons. "I seem to remember that he said something about finding a way in."

"Did any of you see him come out?" Fenris stared at them, his lips thinned to a tight line across his teeth. "Does anyone know for certain that the Gorgons are responsible for this?"

They shifted as they stared at each other but no one spoke.

"Fetch the girl," snapped Fenris. "We'll get to the bottom of this thing now."

He stared at the white-faced girl as she entered, Jarl standing at her side, and she cowered a little at the sight of his stern features.

"You can contact the Gorgons?" He stared at her and slowly she nodded.

"At times I seem to be able to contact them, but mostly they ignore me, only using me as a means of communication with you." Her eyes drifted to the horror in the centre of the room, and Fenris stepped forward, shielding the sight from her gaze.

"Try now," he said. "Try and contact them. I must speak with them, it is important."

She nodded, and closed her eyes, her pale face taking on an even deeper pallor as she concentrated. Abruptly she moaned, swaying a little and resting her hands against her temples.

"You desire to speak with me?" Her voice was cold and utterly inhuman and Fenris knew that it was the strange alien who spoke and not the girl.

"One of the men has had something strange and terrible done to him," he said savagely. "Do you know of this?"

"No."

"You lie! That man was seen entering your section of the ship. Now he is dead, the very bones dissolved in his body. You must know of it."

"I do not know. Yet if you say he entered the forbidden section of the vessel, then his condition is easily explained. There are powerful forces here. Forces too great for you to understand. It may be that he stumbled into one such force and that he paid for his temerity. Remember. You were warned not to enter this section of the vessel and it was no idle warning."

"I see." Fenris glared at the girl and snarled his impatience at not being able to talk to the Gorgons direct. "One other thing. The hull is not absorbing energy fast enough. Why is that?"

"The hull is very old and the energy transmission cycle not as effective as it should be. Also, we have had to use a portion of the collected energy for our own purposes, you will find the accumulators will charge faster now."

"Thanks," said the tall adventurer bitterly. "A fine time to tell us that. Couldn't you have waited until we had charged the ship before drawing on the stored power? Circling the sun isn't the safest thing to do, and it's your lives as well as ours."

"It was essential." The voice spoke with a cold finality and Fenris knew that it was useless to argue.

"Very well. I accept your explanation."

"Do you have further questions?" Somehow the cold voice seemed unutterably weary. "If so ask them now, this means of communication places too great a strain on both myself and the instrument."

"Yes, there is something else. What do we do when the ship has been charged and we have left the area of danger? How do we operate the intra-dimensional controls?"

"That you will leave to us, their operation is far too delicate to trust to your blundering hands. We will know when the time has arrived for their use."

Abruptly the girl staggered and Jarl caught tenderly at her arm. Fenris grinned at the youngster and jerked his head.

"Take her back to her room, see that she has plenty of rest, and Jarl!"

"Yes?"

"Make sure that she doesn't enter the rear section of the ship. Make very sure. Understand?"

The youngster nodded, trying not to stare at the crumpled horror in the centre of the room. He led Lorna to her quarters, and Fenris snapped quick orders to Setter.

"Get them men to clear this mess up. Find a blanket, a sheet, anything and wrap this up and shove it through an airlock. Move now, and remember, none of you are to venture into the rear section of the ship. Just think of what happened to Hammond and you'll know what I mean."

He watched them for a moment then gestured to Branson and waited while the big Captain followed him into the control room. He glanced at the fuel gauge, now registering almost full, stared at the swollen bulk of the sun, then faced the big man.

"Captain, there's something going on that I don't like. Hammond is dead, dead in a particularly horrible manner, and despite what the Gorgons say I believe that they had something to do with it."

"How could they?" Branson adjusted a control then stared at the tall adventurer. "No one dragged Hammond into the rear section of the ship, he must have gone willingly, and it's logical what they say. This is a strange vessel and we can't tell what forces may be operating outside this section. Perhaps some form of radiation did it, perhaps a vibration, anything, we just don't know."

"Admittedly, but Branson, how did he get into that section of the vessel?" Fenris stared at the big man, watching the slow comprehension dawn in the other's eyes. "Exactly. That part of the ship was sealed, sealed from the very moment of take-off. If a door had been left open we'd have found it in our search for the missing man, but there wasn't, and I don't like it."

"You mean that those things deliberately enticed Hammond into their section? But why, Fenris? Why?"

"I don't know, but what has happened has settled it. Branson, do you really want to go on this fantastic journey? If a vibration did that to Hammond, some strange force or radiation, than what might an intra-dimensional shift do to us?"

The big Captain stared at the tall adventurer and his florid face turned pale as he grasped the meaning behind the other's words.

"You think that we'll all die like that?" He shuddered as he remembered the thing that had staggered and screamed and fallen into horrible death. Fenris nodded.

"Why not? It could happen, unless we are a little smarter than those Gorgons give us credit for." He pointed at the flaring visi-screens. "Look, Branson. What's to stop us pulling out of orbit, heading for Earth and landing there? We could turn this ship over to the authorities, claim a free pardon and a cash settlement for salvage, and to hell with those slimy aliens riding in the back. What do you say?"

Branson licked his lips as he thought of it, his eyes glistened with secret hope; then he frowned and shook his head.

"I can't do it, Fenris. They've too much against me, I killed a man once, self-defence but still I killed him, and it would mean prison for life on Jupiter if they ever caught up with me. I daren't land on Earth, and neither dare the crew."

"They'd forget that old crime," insisted Fenris. "Man, with what we've got to offer them they'd wipe out even multiple murder, let alone self-defence. This ship holds all the secrets the Solar Patrol has been looking for over the past twenty years. With it we'd be welcomed with open arms on any planet within the system."

"Maybe you're right," agreed the big Captain. He licked his lips and his eyes held a peculiar expression as they stared at the flickering dials on the control panel.

"Earth," he breathed. "To see the blue sky and the green fields again. To bathe in the sea and listen to the voices of people as they move in the cities. Earth!" He grinned a little shamefacedly at the tall adventurer. "I was born there," he explained. "Haven't set foot on the home world for twenty years now, not since..." He shrugged and stared at his controls.

"You could go back." Fenris rested his hand on the big man's shoulder. "Believe me, Branson, with what this ship contains we'd all be rich men, and we'd do a service for Earth they will always be grateful for."

He turned as Setter stumbled into the control room, the little man's face was strained and his thin lips writhed in a savage wolf-snarl.

"Fenris. You told us to throw Hammond's body out of an air lock."

"Well?"

"Well there isn't any air lock. There isn't even a port or a direct view panel. This ship is sealed and there's no way out! "

"You see." Fenris stared at the big Captain. "We can burn our way out if we have to, but can we do it later on? What do you say, Branson. Do we return?"

"Yes."

Grimly the big man sat at the controls and watched the flaring visi-screens with narrowed eyes. He slid a lever down its groove and needles flickered on dials as energy pulsed into whatever strange engines drove the ship.

"I'm increasing our forward speed," he grunted. "Building up velocity so that we can break out of orbit. It will take a little time, but," he glared at the fuel gauge, "if that instrument means anything we've got plenty of power."

Fenris nodded, then stared at the trembling figure of the little man.

"Now, Setter. What's the trouble?"

"The corpse. We can't get rid of it," babbled the thin faced man. "It's lying there in the big room, a bundle of skin and flesh, and it's getting on my nerves, it's getting on all our nerves. Fenris! You've got to get rid of it!"

"Steady," warned the tall adventurer. "It's only a dead man, surely you've seen enough of them in your time?"

"Maybe I have," snarled the Bosun. "But never before like that. It doesn't look like a dead man should, it looks like a sack of loose flesh, like a thing out of the seas of Venus. I don't like it I tell you, and neither do the men."

Staring down at the shapeless mass Fenris had to agree with the little man. It slumped like a mass of wet dough, like a stranded octopus, like the insane dream of some raving drunkard. The coverings had slipped a little, and a ghastly travesty of a face stared up at the brilliant glow-lights in the roof.

Fenris forced himself to look at it, but he could understand the emotions of the men.

Such a thing shouldn't exist!

The nose was gone of course, a twist of flaccid skin taking its place. The face had spread in a loathsome manner, the eyes slipping from their sockets, and the chin had utterly vanished. It looked like a gargoyle, like a paper mask or a child's creation in putty, but once it had been human, once it had been a living breathing man, and the memory of what it had been made the present reality even more horrible.

"You've got to get rid of it," whispered Setter. "Look at those eyes! Look at them I say! It's still alive, still suffering, kill it!"

"Don't be a fool, Setter!" Fenris snarled at the little man, almost glad of the chance to relieve his own tension. "No man can live without bones. Hammond is dead I tell you, as dead as any man can be!"

"That's what you say," whispered the little man, "but look at those eyes! Look at those eyes!"

"Shut up!" Fenris glared at Setter then jerked his head towards the watching men. "Grab that blanket and pull it against the bulkhead there. Hurry! It can't hurt you now." They glared at him, then edged towards the horrible thing lying on the synthawool blanket. Gingerly they tugged and pulled until it rested against the bulkhead at the rear of the big room, resting against the sealed portion of the vessel. Fenris nodded and slowly drew his gun.

"Since you can't stand to travel with a dead man, and since there's no way in which we can eject him into space, I'll have to cremate him on board." He stared at them, and gestured with the barrel of his heavy weapon.

"Stand back. The heat may be too much for you, it'll probably take several shots and the bulkhead will reflect some of energy."

Deliberately he raised the heavy flare-gun and aimed at the flaccid bulk on the floor before him.

The first shot incinerated the head and the ghastly staring eyes. The second seared half of the remaining bulk and the fourth completed the destruction. Fenris wiped sweat from his face and neck, gasping a little in the hot air, air raised almost to an unbearable temperature by the searing energy from the thundering weapon.

He slipped the flare-gun back into its holster and stared at heat-marked spot where the body had lain. It had gone. Blasted to greasy ash by the incredible power of the flare-gun, the metal of the bulkhead against which it had lain white hot and oozing little streaks of molten metal.

"It's gone," breathed Setter. "Thank Space it's gone!"

"Did you expect it to resist the energy of four charges?" Fenris stared contemptuously at the little man, then staggered as a sudden force gripped the vessel.

"Branson! What's happening?"

He staggered again, then almost slumped to the floor as a thin, high pitched shrilling sound stabbed at his ears with tiny lances of utter pain.

"Branson!"

Desperately he staggered to his feet and lunged towards control room. Beneath his feet the ship seemed to twist a lurch in impossible angles and convoluted curves. He stumbled, almost falling, and still the shrill sound slashed at his ears, jarring his nerves and seeming to burst his brain with shafts of utter agony.

"Branson!"

The big Captain stared from his seat at the controls and florid face was tense and strained with pain. He gestured helplessly towards the controls and his voice was a thin whisper of unbearable pain.

"Fenris. The controls, I can't…"

He groaned and slumped in his padded chair, little trickles of blood rilling from his nose and ears. Painfully the tall adventurer crawled towards the flaring visi-screens, then stared at the looming ball of a familiar planet.

"Mars," he croaked, "but?"

"Couldn't help it," whispered Branson. "The controls didn't answer, someone else operated the ship once we had pulled out of orbit. We seemed to arrive here almost immediately, no chance to stop at Earth, no chance to do anything…"

His voice trailed off into silence and Fenris bit his lips against the shrilling agony of the alien sound.

He knew what it must be. He knew that now their journey had only just begun. The fantastic journey into another dimension, another universe, an unfamiliar plane. He staggered as he left the control room, his hand clawing at the heavy flare-gun at his side, then stopped, his face a mask of agony.

He couldn't make it. He couldn't force his quivering muscles to carry him to the rear of the ship and thankfully he slumped into one of the pilot's chairs.

Before him the visi-screens seemed to blur, the stars to dim and the great bulk of Mars to shift and quiver as if seen through water or a cloud of mist. The shrilling sound had risen higher, higher, until it trembled on the very limit of audibility, then rose even more and silence replaced the shrilling sound.

For a moment there was peace and then...

Fenris shrieked with pain, clawing at his head, his body stiff and rigid in the chair as his feet drummed against the metal of the flooring. He screamed as the super-sonic vibrations tore at the delicate cells of his brain, twisted his nerves into agonised strands and jarred his bones with a sickening torment.

He writhed, praying for death, for unconsciousness, for anything to end the ghastly agony, then it had passed and he slumped in the chair, his entire body streaming with sweat and oozing blood.

A strange sensation replaced the agony. A sensation as if every atom was being vibrated, taken apart and shaken by some microcosmic force, vibrated into a different rhythm from normal. Strange colours and distorted angles flowed across his vision and he seemed to hear the distant murmur of strange machines.

Then he slumped as pain tore at him once more. He twisted writhed, then, as final surcease came, sagged in welcome oblivion.

CHAPTER IX

GORGON REVELATION

It was light and the air was filled with a thin, unfamiliar hum rising and falling, almost hypnotic in its smooth rhythm, and yet, at the same time, somehow alien and vaguely disturbing.

Fenris stirred in the softness of the chair, his eyes flickering open as consciousness and memory returned, and lay for moment listening to the subtly menacing sound.

Branson groaned next to him, and from somewhere in the ship a woman sobbed in a low voice. Fenris jerked himself to his feet, wincing at the pain of his muscles and joints, then grabbed at the back of the padded chair and peered at the distorted lines of the control room.

Somehow it had altered. Somehow the straight lines and smooth surfaces had been transformed to writhing curves and swelling planes. He blinked, rubbing his eyes, and stared again.

The control room remained the same.

He grunted, his hand automatically assuring him that the heavy flare-gun still rested in its holster, then walked stiffly towards the sound of the womanish sobbing.

Lorna looked up at him from where she sat, Jarl's head resting on her lap, and her eyes filled with tears.

"Help me," she sobbed. "Jarl is hurt."

Quickly Fenris dropped on one knee beside them, his strong fingers surprisingly gentle as he probed at the youngster's skull touched the great vein in the throat, and finally lifted one eyelid. He grinned, and ruffled the lad's shock of hair.

"He's not hurt," he said to the girl. "Just sleeping." He stared at the unfamiliar lines of the ship. "What happened?"

"I don't know," she whimpered. "I remember nothing after the first pain, but I think that we must have broken through, I can feel the thoughts of the Gorgons and they are worried."

"Worried?" Fenris stared at her. "Why should they be worried? We've broken through to their own universe haven't we?"

"Yes, but there is something wrong with the ship. I can't read their thoughts, but I know that something is wrong, I can tell it." Abruptly she began to cry again and the tall adventurer shrugged and rose to his feet.

Softly he entered the main living quarters, his pistol ready in his hand, his skin crawling to the sound of the thin humming noise. Something hit his foot and he halted in the middle of a stride. He glanced down, then sprang backwards, a curse in his throat and the heavy weapon thundering in his hand.

Shaft after shaft of searing brilliance stabbed from the pitted orifice, lancing and slashing at the huddled shapes lying on the metal floor.

The flaccid boneless shapes of what had once been men!

Three of them he counted. Three horrible bags of skin and flesh the bones dissolved from their bodies and their white faces awful travesties of what faces should be. Grimly he blasted them, spraying the room with the clean fire of exploding atoms, and not until the last vestige had been burned away did he release his finger from the trigger.

Slowly he reloaded the heavy flare-gun, thrusting fresh charges into the clip, and poising the weapon ready in his hand. His eyes narrowed as he saw an iris opening in the distorted metal of the rear bulkhead, the bulkhead sealing off the

Gorgons section of the vessel, and softly he stepped towards it, the gun a glinting finger of menace in his hand.

Light streamed from the opening, a thin blue luminescence, and with the light came the thin humming noise, shrill, pulsing with some alien rhythm, shocking in its utter suggestiveness and sending little crawling sensations racing along his skin.

Cautiously he peered through the opening.

Cowled figures hunched over strange mechanisms and his flesh crawled as he saw glimpses of white beneath the shielding garments. They clustered around a strange fabrication of crystal and wire, of pulsing energy flows and intricate coils. Light streamed from it and together with that light came the shrilling humming sound.

One of them moved a little, half-turning towards the iris opening, and Fenris ducked back as the metal flowed together to form a seamless wall. He was sweating, and his hand ached from where it gripped the butt of the gun, and he shook as if he had seen something no man should ever see.

He leaned against the wall for a moment, fighting the nausea that churned at his stomach, then grimly straightened himself and began to collect some of thermocans lying scattered about the empty room.

Jarl grinned at him as he passed, and Fenris jerked his head towards the control room.

"Follow me," he snapped. "The girl too. We can talk as we eat."

Branson stared at them as they entered, the big Captain sat limply in the padded chair, his florid face twisted by some inner agony, and the knuckles of his hands gleamed white beneath the skin as he clutched the arms of the chair.

"Fenris," he gasped. "I'm hurt, the vibrations must have churned my guts, broken something inside. I'm sick!"

"Take it easy," said Fenris quietly. He thrust in the tops of several of the cone-shaped thermocans, resting them on the floor while he waited for their contents to heat from the built in chemical units. "You'll feel better after some food." He frowned as he stared around the room. "We're one man short."

"One?" Branson winced as he reached for a steaming thermocan. "Four you mean."

"No, one. I found the other three."

"You did? Where are they?"

"Dead." Fenris stared at their tense faces. "They died the same way as Hammond died. I don't know who is missing, I didn't wait to examine them, just blasted them to ash with the flare-gun." He shuddered and gulped at the vitaminised soup. "I still think those damn Gorgons are responsible for what happened to them. They had left the rear bulkhead open and I peered in. They were working over some weird machine and I almost saw one." He shuddered again, and his strong face paled at the memory. "Luckily I backed away in time."

"What happened?" Jarl stared at the tall adventurer his young face tense and strained. "What can we do now?"

"I don't know," said Fenris slowly. "I think that something must have gone wrong, very wrong, there's a strange alteration in the ship as if it's been caught between dimensions." He looked at the big Captain. "What happened when you broke out of orbit, Captain?"

Branson shrugged.

"I don't rightly know. I'd applied all the power this crate had and we were increasing our velocity to breakaway point. The next thing I knew was that Mars loomed in the visiscreens then that cursed vibration began to twist my guts into knots and I must have passed out."

"Somehow we traversed the distance from the Sun to Mars almost immediately," said Fenris slowly. "That means we must almost have reached the speed of light. The Gorgons took over, that's obvious, but what happened then?"

"The intra-dimensional shift?"

"Yes. That would account for the vibration and the distortion. They must do it by altering the vibratory rate of the sub-atomic particles, that would put us on a different plane, a plane where infra-red for example would register as blue, and radio waves would be something else. I can follow the concepts of that, but what I can't understand is why everything should appear so different, so distorted. If we had come straight through then the ship should look normal."

"Maybe we didn't come straight through," suggested Jarl. "Maybe we stuck halfway?"

"Maybe you've got something there." Fenris stared at the pale face of the young girl.

"Lorna. Try and contact the Gorgons. Try hard. Tell them we must speak with them. Quick!"

She nodded, stiffening into the familiar rigidity and swaying a little as she stood by the head of the padded chair. Jarl caught her, steadying her against his side, and for a long moment they waited as she tried to contact one of the alien creatures.

Nothing happened.

"I can't," she moaned, and her delicate young features twisted with mental agony. "I can't get through."

"Try again," urged Fenris. "Try now."

Again she tried, and again perspiration shone on her face and neck as she tried to contact her alien masters, then she moaned and slumped to the floor. Jarl caught her, his young face tense with worry.

"Blast you, Fenris! Now see what you've done! "

"Forget it," snapped Fenris impatiently. "She'll be all right, just passed out from strain." He thinned his lips and his hand fell to the worn butt of his gun. "If they won't answer when called," he said grimly, "then I'll have to go to them and drag them out." He lifted the heavy flare-gun from its holster and moved steadily towards the door.

Three paces he took, three long strides, then stopped, the gun in his hand swinging level with his waist, then dropping as he remembered the pale blue ray.

A Gorgon stood just within the room.

It was robed and cowled and nothing could be seen of its body, but even so it radiated an aura of menace, and Fenris bit his lips to prevent himself from swinging up the flare-gun and blasting the enigmatic shape with stabbing shafts of searing flame.

He resisted the impulse. Even if he could bring the gun to bear, tighten his finger on the trigger, burn the creature to atomic ash, yet still he must not do it—not yet. Not until he had learned where they were and how to get back home. Killing could come later.

Slowly he replaced the flare-gun in its holster and stared at the cowled figure before him.

"We tried to call you," he said tightly. "What kept you so long?"

"Silence!"

The word burned in his mind, bringing sudden pain, and almost bringing him to his knees with shock and weakness.

"Yes," continued the cold, utterly inhuman, mental voice. "Now it is possible to speak with you direct. On Mars it would not have done to reveal our powers and so we used that pitiful creature you call a female for our instrument. You called you said, what is wrong?"

"That's what we'd like to know," gritted Fenris. "Where are we? What has happened? And why were three men lying dead, their bones dissolved, and their bodies mere bags of skin and flesh? Was that more of your strange energies? Another accident?"

"You mock," whispered the icy voice, "but I do not think that you will mock for long. As for the ship? A slight accident, the burning out of a coil, I told you the vessel was ancient, more ancient than you could imagine, but it will be repaired and soon we shall be home."

"Home?"

"Yes. My home. The world of we whom you call Gorgons. A strange name, why did you pick it?"

"I told you that you had left your mark on legend," said Fenris tightly. "Your paralysing ray gave me the clue and you admitted that you visited Earth. There you were known as 'Gorgons,' what more natural than the name should stick?"

"I remember now," whispered the voice. "The barbarians resisted us, tried to attack the ship, and we had to subdue them. A pity that your world had such a high gravitation, a great pity, but no matter, fresh expeditions can rectify the matter."

"Fresh expeditions?" Fenris stared at the cowled figure. "You mean that this ship was an expedition to explore the worlds of the Solar System?"

"No. The worlds of your vibrational frequency. We were successful in breaking through but the subtle energies met between dimensions ruined our engines. They have not been easy to repair, it was necessary to wait until your peoples had advanced their technology, certain rare metals could not be obtained in the natural state and we did not have the machines necessary to transmute them from common earth."

"You mean that you have waited almost four thousand years? Since the time of the ancient Greeks?"

"The time is nearer five thousand of your years."

The creature seemed almost amused, and Fenris shuddered at the overtones to the alien mirth. "Does that surprise you? Perhaps I should explain that we found rich deposits of a certain rare element on your planet. With it we are potentially immortal."

"I see, then your expedition was successful, but what now? What has happened to the ship?"

"A minor delay, tedious but we shall complete the translation from your universe to our own."

"Complete it? You mean that we are still within our own continuum?"

"Not wholly. The vibrational transition was partially completed. You are not in your own universe but neither are you in mine. We hover between dimensions, but the balance is on your side. Unless the machine is repaired within a certain time, the ship will revert back to your own continuum, but we shall repair it in time."

"I see, and after that?" Fenris licked his dry lips and tried to read the meaning behind the mind-twisting mental voice. "You promised us great rewards."

"I did?"

"Yes. I would like this ship as payment for what we have done for you. Naturally we shall have to be transported back to our own continuum, and so we may as well retain the ship which takes us."

"Indeed?" Almost it seemed the eerie voice laughed with alien humour and Fenris felt sweat start out in great beads on his face and neck.

"You made a bargain," he said grimly. "I want you to keep it."

"Fool!" The mental voice turned savage, seeming to snarl and beating them to their knees with its sheer brain-wrenching impact. "You made a bargain? You! How can cattle bargain with their superiors? We needed you, needed you as proof of the rich deposits we had found, and when we deliver you to our people great will be our fame and our reward. You will never return to your pitiful planet. You will not return, but we will. Return in force with ships and weapons to bring your animal-like peoples to their knees. We shall rule and you shall be our cattle. That was long decided, and but for a trivial accident, would have long been the fashion. Speak no more of return!"

"I guessed it!" Fenris stared at the thing and his hand twitched over the butt of his gun. "You speak of us as cattle? Why?"

"I mentioned certain deposits of rare elements, elements which will assure us immortality. Those deposits are in your bones. Now do you understand?"

The voice died and the creature vanished into the rear portion of the ship.

Fenris cursed weakly as he clawed at his gun.

CHAPTER X

THE MISSING MAN RETURNS

Cattle!

They thought about it as they drank their vitaminised soup and stared at the blurred streaks in the visi-screens. They thought about it as they waited for the Gorgons to repair the damaged engines, and they thought about it as they checked and rechecked the heavy flare-guns at their waists.

They thought about it, and they thought of Hammond and the way he had died, the three men lying like sacks of skin and flaccid flesh, and desperation gnawed deep within them as they thought of Earth and the menace hovering over the home world. Branson put it into words.

The big man sat slumped in his chair, deep lines of pain tracing their path across his scarred features and a thin trickle of blood rilling from his twisted mouth.

"We've got to stop them, Fenris. Got to!"

"How?" The tall adventurer shrugged and finished his examination of his heavy pistol. "You think that I don't know that? Man! Once these creatures carry the word to their own planet that immortality is to be found on Earth, there'll be no stopping them. Remember the weapons we used on the attacking patrol ships? Remember the metal of the outer hull? We wouldn't stand a chance against them."

"We've got to stop them," repeated the big Captain stubbornly, and Fenris nodded.

"I agree. We'll never be able to do it once they arm and attack Earth so we must do it now." He frowned, staring down at the flare-gun and biting his lips in deep thought. "If we can somehow kill them while we're still stranded between these dimensions the ship will revert back to our own continuum. That thing told us that, so the problem is really a simple one, how can we stop them repairing the ship?"

"Kill them," said the Captain, and spat a mouthful of blood.

"Kill them," said Jarl, his young face white as he thought of the horror waiting to engulf Earth.

"Kill them?" Fenris smiled and gently shook his head. "I tried that once, back on Mars when I wanted to throw a container of wine at one and crush it to a pulp. Do you remember what happened then?"

"The paralysis beam?" Branson nodded. "What of it? Paralysis ray, flare-gun, knife, they're all weapons, none of them can do more than kill a man, that's a risk we'll have to take."

"A risk yes, but it isn't the same. With a knife or flare-gun a man can take a wound and still be able to shoot back. No matter what happens he stands a chance of killing his enemy, but not with the paralysis cay. I've felt it and I know. They wouldn't want to kill us anyway, we're too valuable to prove to their rulers what is to be found on Earth."

Impatiently the tall adventurer strode about the narrow confines of the control room.

"Jarl. Search the ship, see if you can find the missing man. Lorna. Try and remember everything you can about the Gorgons, you've lived with them for so long that you must have picked up something that may be of use. Branson. What chance do we have of blasting away from this sector of space?"

"None." The big Captain shook his head as he stared at the controls. "They must have disengaged this set from the true controls, we have no power over the ship now, haven't had since we broke away from the Sun."

Fenris shrugged and stared at the white face of Jarl. The youngster shook his head.

"Nothing. We're the only living things in this part of the ship."

"Then where is the missing man?" Fenris stood, his eyes blank with deep thought, then nodded, a sick expression on his face.

"There's only one place he could be, in the rear part of the ship, with the Gorgons. Poor devil! "

"Why do you say that?" Branson stared at the tall adventurer, then swallowed, and slowly shook his head. "I see what you mean." He clenched his big hands and the scar tissue on his cheek flamed against the strained pallor of his features. "Fenris! We've got to do something!"

"I know it, but what?" The tall adventurer glanced at the white-faced girl. "Lorna. Have you thought of anything yet?"

"No."

"Are you certain? Anything, any little scrap of knowledge would help us now."

"There is nothing. I stayed with the old Martians most of the time, the Gorgons only used me to communicate to others, and saw little of them other than when they needed me. There was one thing though."

"Yes?"

"Sometimes the Martians would appear worried, angry rather, I never did see one of them in a real temper. It happened after the Gorgons used to call several of them into their hidden quarters, and for a long while after that I never used to see the Gorgons at all. It was as if they were sleeping or resting. Does that help at all?"

"Perhaps." Fenris stared at her, his face tense. "Lorna. How many Gorgons are there?"

"Four."

"Are you certain?"

"Yes."

"Now I begin to understand." He stared at them and tightened his lips into a thin smile. "If we were explorers, as the Gorgons are, and we had found something of rare value, as they did. What would be the logical thing to do?"

"Carry back specimens," grunted Branson.

"Exactly, but assume that what we carried would give us potential immortality, what then?"

"I see what you mean." The big Captain stared at the tall adventurer and nodded. "They would return with specimens of course, but they would also make certain that they themselves acquired immortality."

"Exactly!" Fenris nodded. "They have saved their specimens, a young pair, one male one female so that they can increase the stock. Two big, fully grown males for research and use." He grinned without humour. "I wonder how much of their rare element they will find in our bones, Branson? How many extra years of life will we give to those slimy aliens?"

"Don't!" gasped the big Captain. "I can't bear to think about it."

"That accounts for the others," mused Fenris quietly.

"Hammond must have been used as a test, perhaps they weren't certain that their machines would work, or perhaps they just got plain greedy. Anyway he was shared between them, and we know what happened to him. Then we began the intra-dimensional shift. The things may have felt a little worried, perhaps they didn't feel like relying on the generosity of their rulers, or perhaps it was just an elementary precaution, but they decided to stock up with the rare element. They selected one man each, that still left us four as specimens, and three of them must have eaten. I saw the remains of their meal."

He stared at the others and noticed their dawning stares of comprehension.

"Yes. Three of them have eaten and so are in a state of coma, or perhaps they are like the big snakes of Earth, they have to rest for a time while their bodies assimilate the rare element from the bones of the men they killed." He paused, and his eyes glittered in the dim light reflected from the blurred visi-screens. "Will the remaining thing wait before making certain that he has his share of immortality?"

"No." Branson shook his head, deep lines of pain running from nose to mouth, and his lips red with blood from his internal wounds.

"They will repair the ship first. Why hurry when they have plenty of time and the knowledge that they can always get more supplies of their rare element."

"You are wrong, Branson," said Fenris quietly. "How can you even guess at the lure of immortality? You can't, and neither can I, but I can guess what must happen. They have waited five thousand years to return home, what matter if they wait another five? They have eternal life, Branson! They can afford to wait before repairing the vessel—but can they dare wait to restore their immortality?"

He stared at them and the thin line of his mouth showed against the tenseness of his tight drawn features.

"That thing in there must be busy. Its companions are comatose, bloated with their foul meal, stuffed with the rare element sucked from the bones of living men. Three of them are sure of many more years of life to come, can the fourth one resist the lure? I say not. Even now it must be feeding on the missing man. That means that it will be preoccupied, intent on what it is doing, careless of outside interference. We must take advantage of this moment. If we are to attack at all, then now is the time to do it!"

Branson nodded, heaving himself painfully out of the padded chair, and breathing in gasping wheezes as he clawed himself upright.

"I'm with you," he muttered, and dragged the heavy flare-gun from the holster at his waist.

"I'm with you." Jarl stepped forward from where he stood beside the slender figure of the girl. His young face was pale and his hands trembled a little, but he drew his weapon with a grim assurance, and his eyes were bright.

"No, Jarl." Fenris shook his head. "You stay here. What has to be done can be done by Branson and me. You have other things to worry about."

"What are they, Fenris?"

"The girl. Should we fail would you like to see her a prisoner of the Gorgons? A piece of cattle valuable only for the bones in her body and the young she could bear?"

"No!"

"Then stay here beside her. If we fail you know what you must do."

He stared at the too-white face of the lad, and grinned with false humour at the wondering features of the girl. Branson groaned a little, swaying as he gripped the head of the padded chair, and Fenris knew that the big man was dying as he stood. Gently he took the Captain's arm and together they walked towards the rear of the ship.

It was sealed, the strange sheen of the alien metal unmarked by any trace of an opening, and Fenris thinned his lips as he stared at it.

"We'll have to burn it open, Branson. Aim at a point directly ahead, about waist high, where the metal is marked by the energy of my shots when I burned Hammond's body. Together now, ready! "

"Ready," whispered the big Captain, and his thick fingers tightened on the trigger of his heavy flare-gun. Flame spouted from the pitted orifice. A thin streak of searing energy thundering and blasting at the stubborn metal before them. Splashing on the smooth surface and sending reflected heat lashing back at the two men.

"Wait." Fenris stared at the dully glowing spot on the stubborn bulkhead and wiped sweat from his streaming features. "We need a shield, something to protect us from the reflected radiations." He turned, almost running from the big room, and when he returned he held a wide section of polished metal.

"Cut it from the control housing," he explained. "Get behind it and fire around the edge. Use your charge, then reload, and take over from me. Ready?"

"Yes."

Carefully the big Captain squeezed the trigger of his flare-gun. Thunder echoed through the room, the roaring thunder of exploding atoms, and the air steamed and grew painful to breathe as the released energy slashed at the glowing metal of the bulkhead and was reflected back into the room.

Again and again the big Captain fired the heavy pistol, squeezing the trigger until the charges were exhausted and the orifice of the gun shimmered, almost incandescent with heat.

Grimly Fenris took over, blasting charge after charge against the softening metal of the alien ship. Slowly it began to yield beneath the tremendous barrage, turning from red to yellow, from yellow to white, from white to scintillant blue. Then great droplets of molten metal oozed from the central point and slowly an opening gaped in the once-smooth bulkhead.

"Hold it!" Fenris squinted at the opening, his fingers blistering as he thrust fresh charges into the butt of his gun. "Wait a moment, let it cool off, I want to take a look in there." Branson nodded, his weapon hanging from one listless hand, his mouth and chin red with the blood from his internal injuries. Cautiously he approached the opening.

Heat seared his skin from the still-molten metal and his lungs burned as he gulped the hot air, but he ignored the physical discomforts, staring into the sealed portion of the ship, his eyes wide with sudden loathing.

The thin humming noise still whined from the strange machine and the blue pulsations of the alien energy-flow ebbed and grew in the intricate coils. Fenris stared at the machine, his eyes thoughtful, then he smashed it to tinkling dust and fuming vapour with one shot from the heavy pistol in his hand.

The roar of the discharge died into silence, and from the dimness at the rear of the ship, something moved.

It staggered, a mass of white skin and sagging flesh. It whimpered its hands clawing before it and two eyes staring horribly from the distorted planes of its face. It hopped, trying to walk on legs that could no longer stand its weight and its arms writhed in a horrible tentacular fashion.

"What is it?" Branson stared and then doubled in a terrible fit of vomiting. Fenris swallowed, fighting the terror clawing at his mind and the sickness tearing at his stomach. The thing hopped nearer and now the tall adventurer could see the indescribable look of horror on its face.

"The missing man," he whispered. "God! That thing is the missing man!"

"Kill it! Burn it down! Get rid of it, quick!" Branson retched again then groaned as blood rilled from his open mouth. He staggered, almost falling, then twisted, the flare-gun in his hand steadying on the pale horror advancing towards them.

Fire lashed from the gun. A streak of scintillant energy, destroying, burning, cleansing with its atomic flame. The thing stopped, swayed, then sagged to the metal of the floor, its head a blackened ember, and its unnatural life wiped out in the heat of the discharge.

Something moved at the rear of the ship. Fenris stared at it, then, as instinct screamed its warning, ducked back into the room.

A pale ray of clearest blue lanced through the burned out opening.

CHAPTER XI

BRANSON'S SACRIFICE

It wavered for a second, reflecting from the polished surface of the walls, and as it passed, Fenris felt the numbing effect of the paralysis beam. Branson moaned in agony from where he leaned against the wall and Fenris stared at him with worried eyes.

"How is it, Branson? Can you hold out for a while longer?"

"I don't know." The big Captain wiped blood from his mouth and stared at the back of his red-stained hand. "The pain is killing me, I must be bleeding to death inside; I don't think I can last much longer, Fenris."

Again the pale blue ray leaped and quivered about the room, and watching it, the tall adventurer frowned in mental torment.

"They're awake," he said bitterly. "Soon they'll be coming out here."

"I hope that they do," whispered the big Captain. "Fenris, do you think that man I shot was Setter?"

"Could be. Why?"

"We were friends him and me, good friends. I wouldn't like to think that I shot him down like a dog. Was it him do you think?"

"If it was you did him a favour," said the tall adventurer gently. "He was dying, his bones collapsing beneath his own weight, and he knew it! Those Gorgons must somehow extract one of the binding materials from human bone, the result is just as if they had dissolved the calcium leaving nothing but a useless dust or thin fluid. I don't know who that man was, but I know this, if I was in his condition I'd bless the man with guts enough to burn me down."

"Thanks, Fenris, you make me feel a lot better." Branson straightened against the wall, the flare-gun steadying in his hand. "How long are they going to keep us waiting? I don't think I can last much longer and I want to take some of those slimy devils with me."

"Take it easy," warned the young man. "I've ruined their engine and all we have to do now is to wait until we're drawn back to our own continuum. The longer we can hold them off the better."

"I can't wait that long!" Branson heaved himself away from the wall, his face a mask of hate and pain. "Fenris. Suppose I go in there, blast whatever I can, shoot at anything at all, would that do any good?"

"You'd never pull the trigger," Fenris snapped. "That ray would freeze you to stone and you'd be dead before you knew it. No, Branson, you'd only throw your life away."

"What's the difference, I'm as good as dead now." Grimly the Branson staggered towards the blue-lit opening. "I'm going to try it, Fenris, don't try and stop me!"

"Wait!"

The tall adventurer bit his lip as he stared at the big Captain. Branson meant every word he had said, and to stop him was to invite quick death. The man was half-mad with pain and despair, filled with murderous rage and the killing instinct, and he had room for only one thought at a time.

To kill the Gorgons!

Nothing but death would stop him. No friend, no argument, nothing. Fenris knew it, and knew that he had no right to determine how any man should choose the manner of his death.

"I'll help you, Branson," he said quickly. "Wait for just a moment."

"No." Branson shook his head. "No need for us both a die. You stay here, when I fail, if I fail, then you must try again. Stand back now."

"Hold it I tell you!" Impatient anger edged the young man's voice, and the big Captain hesitated, hovering at the edge of the blue-lit opening.

"Well?"

"Set your gun for continuous fire. Here I'll do it for you." Fenris snatched the weapon and his fingers moved with a peculiar skill as he adjusted the internal setting of the firing chamber. He snapped the insulation shut and handed back the flare-gun.

"When you press the trigger it will blast a continuous stream of flame. It won't last long of course, the chamber will probably explode or the barrel fuse, but it will last long enough."

"Good. Goodbye, Fenris."

"Blast you man can't you wait a second! "

"What now?" The big Captain swayed and blood frothed at his lips from his internal injuries. "Hurry man! I'm almost dead!"

"I'll fire around the edge of the opening, try and make them aim their rays towards me. You press the trigger of the gun, stick it through the opening, and traverse the entire room." He hesitated, then bit his lip as he saw the grey face of the dying man.

"Good luck, Captain. See you in Hell."

"Yes," whispered the big man, and pressing the trigger stepped directly into the opening.

Fenris crouched to one side, the barrel of his weapon blasting fire into the rear of the vessel. His hand grew cold, the flare-gun falling from his numb fingers as a ray lashed across his hand. He cursed, staggering back, and watched the big Captain as he rubbed life back into his paralysed fingers.

Branson was dead.

He stood just within the opening, the flare gun roaring continuous song of destruction as it emptied itself into the rear of the vessel, and around his big body flickered the lambent rays of clear blue death.

They had killed the big man. Stopped his heart and frozen his brain, but still he remained on his feet, a fixed snarl on his blood-stained mouth and the thundering pistol in his hand swept a path of destruction as he slowly spun and toppled to the metal floor.

He fell, and together with his falling the spouting flare-gun reddened, grew molten, then exploded with a flare and gush of searing heat.

When Fenris opened his eyes nothing remained of the big Captain but ash and dust and a glowing spot on the floor.

But from the rear of the alien ship echoed the thin shrilling of unhuman screams.

Fenris snarled as his hand slowly returned to life. He scooped up his pistol and cautiously peered over the ragged edge of the burned out opening. Something white drifted among the blasted ruin of what had once been machines. Something pale and horrible, moving with a sinuous grace and radiating a mind-chilling aura of primeval horror.

Fenris gulped and jerked his head from the opening just as a pale blue light streamed towards him from the alien being.

He gulped, feeling a terrible sickness welling inside him, sickness born of twisted senses and disrupted neuron paths in his brain. The Gorgons were horrible, not so much with the physical appearance, but the very radiations of their alien minds registered on the human brain as fear and terror and utter loathing.

The Gorgons had to die!

Fenris sagged by the thin wall between him and sanity, knowing that sooner than let them take him alive he would blast his head to smouldering ash. He stared about the room, feeling the insidious numbing effect of the reflected paralysis rays, and his lips thinned to a humourless smile as he stared at the polished sheet of metal he had torn from the control housing.

A shield!

Something to reflect the deadly rays, to act as a mirror so that he could see where to aim his destroying blasts of searing energy. He snatched it, turning it and staring into the smooth surface, trying to orient himself to the unfamiliar angle of reflection.

Desperately he struggled with the sheet of thin metal, trying to force both hand and eye into strange habit patterns, staring at the polished metal and aiming his heavy gun, not at where he stared, but at what he saw. It was hard, too hard, and he cursed as he half-heard, half-sensed, the whispering shuffle of alien feet.

The Gorgons were coming to end the battle!

Desperately he crouched in a corner, well away from the opening, the thin metal propped against the angle of the wall and twisted so that while protecting him, it also threw its image onto the polished steel of the bulkhead. He squinted at the dim reflection, tilting the shield so that it threw the image of the opening onto the wall, then twisting his hand and arm so that his flare-gun pointed towards the burned out opening.

Tensely he waited.

He waited while ice-fingers traced a pattern on his naked brain, while his nerves jumped and twisted and his blistered skin burned to the salty sweat streaming from every pore. He waited, and as he waited, odd scraps of half-forgotten knowledge came tumbling into his fevered brain.

The Gorgons! They had visited Earth in the dim and distant past, and there they had left their mark on legend. The old Greeks had fought them, fought them with swords and spears, with naked fists and unbelievable courage, but they had beaten off those old armies, frozen them where they stood with the power of the blue ray, the paralysing beam which had turned men to stone.

Something clicked just within the opening, and Fenris tensed, his hand aching from gripping the butt of his gun. His arm burned with fatigue and his shoulder muscles felt as if they would break as he crouched in his unnatural posture, but he knew that to move would mean quick and horrible death, so he sat, great beads of sweat streaming down his face, and waited for the enemy.

This wasn't the first time, he thought grimly. Someone else had fought with them just as he was doing now. Some old hero armed with a sword and shield. Legend told the story, but legend was always overlaid with too much wishful thinking and the truth was buried beneath layers of mouth-to-mouth exaggeration. He wished that the aliens would hurry.

The clicking came again, louder this time, and then...

Something white and tentacular and utterly horrible slid through the opening. It was an unholy union of beast and insect, of things that should have remained in the depths of the sea, and things that screamed at men from twisted nightmares. It hesitated, the clustered organs on its truncated top waving a little as they searched the room.

From them shot the blue ray!

Fenris bit his lips until the blood ran down his chin, digging teeth into the torn flesh and fighting his every instinct which told him to get up and run, run, run and keep on running until he fell in utter exhaustion.

A second Gorgon joined the first!

They saw him then, saw the sheet of polished metal propped at an odd angle in one corner, and must have guessed what lay behind it. From the writhing tentacles crowning their truncated upper portions the blue rays spat, streaming towards the shield metal and the reflecting walls.

Fenris grew numb.

He crouched behind the thin sheet of polished metal, his eyes bulging in his head as he stared at the dim reflection in the wall before him. His arm ached as he shifted the heavy weight of the flare-gun, shifted it to align on the dim figures limned on the metal wall.

Desperately he pulled the trigger.

Flame blasted from the weapon, a searing blast of brilliant energy, and one of the things screamed in a thin shrilling alien voice.

Again he fired. Again, squeezing the trigger and sending gouts of blasting destruction flaring across the opening, across the twin heaps of charred tissue, sweeping the area clean with the released energy of exploding atoms.

When the gun was empty he stopped squeezing the trigger.

He rose from behind his shield, the thin sheet of metal which had protected him from the organic ray of the paralysing beam, and fumbled with burnt fingers as he reloaded the flare-gun. Deliberately he stepped through the opening into the rear of the ship, knowing that if he didn't do it now he would never be able to do it later.

Twice more he used the gun. Sending stabbing shafts of destruction into two loathsome objects already burned almost in two.

Then he headed for the familiar safety of the control room.

Jarl caught him as he entered, helping him to one of the padded chairs, his young face tense with worry and unspoken questions.

"It's over." Fenris winced as he massaged his burned hands. "Branson is dead, he died like a hero. The Gorgons are dead, they died like the slimy rats they are. The ship will revert back to our own continuum, when I don't know, but it shouldn't take long." He smiled at the anxious face of the girl.

"Don't worry, Lorna. We'll all be rich when we turn this ship over to the scientists, and Jarl will look after you, won't you Jarl?"

He smiled at the youngster's expression, then slumped back in the padded seat as he waited for the blurred visi-screens to clear and for Mars to loom, red and familiar, close to them.

The ships would come then, the patrol ships of Mars, and they would be safe among familiar things.

He frowned, half drifting on the edge of sleep, and he kept a resolve to the front of his relaxed mind.

He would have to find out the name of that old hero.

SECOND FROM THE SUN

If Dolman had been completely sober he would have been suspicious, but he was just drunk enough to look on any Earthman as a friend. Even such a wizened, rat-faced individual who accosted him in Madam Zen's thil joint in the free quarter of Venusburg.

"Molton," said the stranger. "Carl Molton. You'll drink with me?"

"Why not?" Dolman, his ripped shirt revealing a barrel torso, shrugged easy acceptance. Even though the fumes of thil had risen to his head he hadn't quite lost all caution. Molton was tanned, neatly and cleanly dressed and was obviously a new arrival who hadn't yet been bleached and worn by the sunless skies and humidity of Venus. He could have been a tourist with more money than sense out on a slumming spree. He wasn't; his face didn't fit the role and neither did the way he carried himself. He radiated assurance and a certain ruthless hardness. Dolman had met men like him before.

A scaled Hotlander brought two beakers to the table, hissed politely as Molton threw him a coin and backed sinuously away.

"Here's health." Molton lifted his beaker and sipped at the contents.

"Clear jets." Dolman gulped half the thil, a little of the thin, green wine running down over his chin. He wiped it with his hand, staring at the other's barely touched drink. "Don't you like it?"

"I've had worse." Molton sipped again. "Your name's Dolman, isn't it? Pat Dolman?"

"That's right." Dolman swallowed the rest of his wine.

"I've heard of you." Over the rim of his beaker Molton's eyes were hard and shrewd. "Lone survivor of the *Evening Star.* Was found wandering in the Hotlands, stood trial and was busted from the SS." He sipped again. "How long ago now? A year?"

"You know a lot," said Dolman tightly. He shook his head against the thickening fumes of the wine. "Maybe it would be a good idea to keep it to yourself."

"Maybe it would," agreed Molton. He looked at Dolman's empty beaker. "More thil?" He snapped his fingers at the waiter.

Dolman started to protest, then relaxed as gourd-drums sounded their rattling beat. At one end of the tavern a girl spun onto the floor with a glitter of crystal and a swirl of cobwebs. She was a Highlander, a tall albino with long, white hair as fine as gossamer. Her eyes were pink and her skin almost translucent. Molton stared at her, then glanced at Dolman.

"Nice dish," he said. "Local?"

"A Highlander. She comes from the mountains."

"A native?" Molton seemed surprised. "She looks Terrestrial to me."

"She is." Dolman didn't take his eyes from the writhing figure of the girl. "A long time ago her folks came from Earth. Or maybe it was the other way around and her folks colonized Earth. Aside from the albinoism the Highlanders are just the same as we are." He fumbled for the beaker of thil and drank, his eyes concentrated on the dancer.

She was dancing the Dance of Endearment and in Madam Zen's that was a foolish thing to do. The dyed garments spun from the webs of giant spiders did little to conceal the lithe lines of her body. The crystal ornaments flashed and glittered in the light of the flaring lanterns and the incessant rattling of the gourd-drums was like needles scratching at nerves. Men began to shift restlessly on their chairs, gulping at their thil and drinking in the beauty of the dancer with eyes which matched the glitter of her ornaments. A burly tubeman cursed as a waiter moved before him, spoiling his view. The curse turned into action as he swept the scaled Hotlander aside with one thick arm. A tavern girl screamed as the waiter sprang forward his claws extended and reaching for the tubeman's face.

Dolman saw none of the fight which followed. He sat as if entranced, his eyes filled with the shifting glitter of moving crystal, his head fogged with the mounting fumes of thil. The fumes grew thicker, the glitter seemed to fade in a closing mist and then, like a host of stars, fell away as the blackness closed around him.

He woke with a pain behind his eyes, a sour taste in his mouth and the uneasy conviction that he didn't know where he was. The headache and furred teeth were familiar; he?d suffered from hangovers before. The lack of orientation was familiar, too, but for that he'd long ago worked out a routine. Without moving or altering the tempo of his breathing he cautiously opened his eyes.

He stared at a criss-cross of thin metal straps. They were backed by something dark and didn't offer any help. To his right was a metal wall, to his left an open space lit by a peculiar blue glow. The glow worried him. It came from standard tube lights, was rich in ultra violet and was as familiar as his hangover.

Dolman swore, sat upright and swore again as he cracked his head on the bottom of the bunk above. Carefully, he slid long legs to a metal floor and stood up, fighting the waves of nausea which drained his strength. Weakly he stumbled to a chair and sat down, elbows resting on a table, hands supporting his throbbing head. He looked up as a door clicked open and a man entered the room. It was Molton.

"So you're awake," he said. "How do you feel?"

"Terrible." Dolman ran his tongue around his mouth. "Where are we?"

"In a cabin at the edge of the Hotlands." The wizened man crossed to a cabinet, worked at something Dolman couldn't see and returned with a beaker of some foaming liquid. "Drink this, it'll settle you."

"Thanks." Dolman gulped the drink and rested his head on his hands again. His first worry had vanished; he was not in a spaceship. Tube lights were standard equipment in the metal coffins in which men rode between the planets but rarely found elsewhere. He began to change his mind about Molton; the tan meant nothing now, the man could have been on Venus for years.

"Better?" Molton looked at his fingernails.

"I think so." Dolman cautiously lifted his head. The pain behind his eyes had vanished and so had the furriness around his teeth. There was a taint left in his mouth though, a peculiar metallic taste which he hadn't noticed before. He stared thoughtfully at the other man. "What happened?"

"You got drunk," said Molton easily. "Someone started a fight and I got you away and brought you here." He chuckled. "It wasn't easy; you're a big man."

"That's right," reminded Dolman. "I am, aren't I?" He openedand closed his right hand. "Big enough, I'd say, to be able to throttle you with one hand. Or to break your neck."

"If I were to let you." Molton suspended the examination of his manicure. "But why would you want to do that?"

"I don't like to be kidnapped. And I don't like to be drugged." He smiled without humour. "I've drunk too much thil not to have learned my capacity. And I could write a book on thil hangovers. You drugged me back at Madam Zen's. Why?"

"Can't you guess?" Molton, Dolman noticed, didn't trouble to deny the accusation. Instead, he sat and stared at the big man with a peculiar intentness.

"You want something," said Dolman. "From me. Right?"

"Yes." Molton rested his hand at his waist. "Before you start getting any foolish ideas let me inform you that this cabin is two hundred miles from Venusburg. We arrived by helicopter which has since left. There is no Hotland equipment in this place. You might be able to kill me, but if you do you'll be stuck here."

"I wasn't thinking of killing you," said Dolman mildly. "Now suppose we stop wasting time and get down to business?"

"You were first officer on the *Evening Star*," said Molton abruptly. "You can begin by telling me just what happened."

"About the crash?" Dolman shrugged and fumbled in his pockets. Molton threw a package of cigarettes on the table and the big man lit one, inhaling deeply, his craggy face sombre as he let smoke trickle from his nostrils. "We took off from Venusburg on the regular schedule for Earth," he said abruptly. "We were climbing on the beacon when, at about a hundred and fifty miles, our reactors blew up." He noticed the other man's expression. "I mean that literally. One moment they were operating at full efficiency, the next they were just fused junk and we were coming down again—fast."

"That's what you said at the trial." Molton helped himself to a cigarette. "The examining officers didn't believe you, why should I?"

"I don't care a damn if you believe me or not, that's what happened." Dolman dragged at his cigarette. "What happened next, happened fast. I was on duty at the time and when we started to fall I hit the emergency crash button. We jettisoned fuel, dumped the pile and shed cargo. The parachutes opened and we smacked down in the Hotlands." He looked at the cigarette. "The engine crew went out with the reactors. The second and third officers died in the crash. The captain, doctor and myself managed to crawl out of the wreckage. Together we tried to make it through the jungle to Venusburg. The others didn't make it."

"And you were found by a search party raving with fever and suffering from shock, bums and loss of memory." Molton nodded. "I told you that I'd attended the trial."

"Then why ask me what you already know?"

"The *Everting Star* was a cargo ship carrying goods to Earth," said Molton slowly. "Those goods have never been recovered."

"I told you that we dumped the cargo."

"I know. I also know that three search parties went out looking for it. They didn't find it."

"So?"

"So you are the only survivor," said Molton slowly. "The search parties had to depend on you for their co-ordinates. They only had your word for it that the cargo was dumped where you claimed." He leaned back in his chair. "That was a pretty important cargo, Dolman."

"All cargo is important."

"This more than most." Molton flicked ash from his cigarette. "At the trial you were found guilty of negligence and kicked out of the Spacial Service. For the past year you've been hanging around the free quarter. You're an intelligent man, Dolman, too intelligent perhaps for your own good."

"Keep talking," said Dolman. His eyes were hard and a muscle jumped high on his left cheek.

"A smart officer might recognise an opportunity when he saw it. He could, shall we say, have conveniently forgotten to give the correct co-ordinates to the search parties. He could, in fact, have some idea of salvaging that dropped cargo for himself." Molton crushed out his cigarette. "That cargo is worth a quarter of a million credits," he said casually.

"It was insured for three million."

"I was speaking of its personal value to you. A quarter of a million credits—if you will guide a party to where it is to be found."

"I see." Dolman frowned at the coil of smoke rising from his cigarette. It began to add up, the meeting at Madam Zen's, the drugged thil, the strange awakening in this hidden cabin.

"A quarter of a million is a lot of money," said Molton. "It would buy you passage to anywhere in the System and set you up wherever you choose. You would be rich and independent for the rest of your life."

"I'm not arguing."

"Of course not. I said that you were an intelligent man." Molton lit a fresh cigarette. "I'll make arrangements for us to start at once. We'll travel as a hunting party with you as our guide. You'll have to stay here for a little while, but you'll find all you need in the cabinets. There's a shower through that door and vids and projector in that box."

"And thil?"

"No thil. This trip you stay sober." Molton rose and stepped towards the door. Dolman called to him as he reached the panel.

"When do I meet the big boss?"

"You've met him."

"And the money, when do I get that?"

"After we have found the cargo." Molton smiled again. "You will have to trust me," he said gently. "Surely you can see that?"

"I have no alternative." Dolman had one more question. "Supposing I had refused to co-operate?"

"You had no alternative to that, either." Molton didn't elaborate, and he didn't have to. His meaning was plain.

The expedition consisted of Molton, two hard-faced men called Sam and Mike, a fat, wheezing individual the others called Doc, and a girl. Dolman took one look at her, then protested to Molton.

"I'm sorry," said the wizened man. "Miss Conroy will have to accompany us."

"Are you crazy?" Dolman shook his head in bafflement. "This isn't a picnic we're going on. The Hotlands are tough, too tough for most men and any woman." He scowled at the girl where she sat at the far end of the cabin. She wore light-weight tropical gear which did nothing to diminish her figure. Her hair was blonde, she was tanned from exposure to the unshielded sun and seemed to carry with her a breath of Earth.

"Shelia is important to our mission," said Molton. "She is more capable than she looks and will prove no burden." He changed the subject. "I've arranged for the hire of a helicopter. Doc is a qualified pilot and will attend to the machine."

"I could have done that."

"I know, but we may need you for other duties." He hesitated. "If you will just give him the co-ordinates?"

"Once I do that then I won't be needed," reminded Dolman. "And I wouldn't say that you were the type of man to hesitate to earn a quarter million for the sake of a shot in the back."

"We must trust each other." Molton wasn't annoyed.

"I trust you," said Dolman. "But only as far as I have to." He got down to business. "I shed the cargo north of the Jagged Mountains; that's the big range between Venusburg and Aphrodite. We were travelling fast so you can realize that I didn't have much time to take exact co-ordinates. That country's pretty rough and the containers fell into the jungle." He took a chart from his pocket. "The area was about here." His finger tapped a patch of white. "Unexplored country like most of Venus. The only thing we can be sure about is that it's teeming with dangers."

"The containers were fitted with radiation tags, of course?"

"I suppose so, they usually are, but the range is short and the background radiation pretty high. You'll have to get close before you can pick up their signal." Dolman folded the chart. "So we'll head there, make camp and use the helicopter in a search-pattern."

"Will we be able to spot the place it landed from the air?" Molton looked confused. "It would have broken a patch on landing, wouldn't it?"

"Sure, and the jungle would have grown back within days." Molton, obviously, knew less i about Venus than he should have. Or he was keeping up a pretence?

Dolman didn't know, but during the trip to the camp site he had plenty of time to think about it. Plenty of time too to think about the girl. The cabin was packed with the essential gear for life in the Hotlands, and he found himself sitting next to her. His interest wasn't returned.

"First trip to Venus, Shelia?"

"Yes, Mr. Dolman." She had brought some of the Arctic in her voice. He tried again.

"Molton a friend of yours?"

"Yes."

"And old friend?" It seemed impossible that this girl had a criminal bent. Dolman had met the fringe crowd too often during the past year and he knew the signs. This girl had none of them. Either she was a perfect actress or didn't know just what was going on.

"I suggest you ask Mr. Molton about that." She turned and stared at him. "I would also suggest that you stop bothering me."

"And if I don't take your suggestion?"

"You'll take it, bud." Sam, one of the hard-faced couple, leaned forward and touched his knee. "You'll take it or you'll get hurt."

"You think so?" Dolman smiled but it was the smile of a tiger. Molton saw it.

"I think Doc could do with you, Dolman," he called. "We must be getting near the camp site now."

Dolman hesitated, then crawled towards the pilot's seat. Doc, despite his fat and wheeze, was an excellent pilot. He kept the machine flying just above the tree tops for, as Dolman guessed, maximum invisibility from interested parties.

"We've about reached where you said." Doc caressed the controls as a tug-bird dashed itself to death against the plastic before him. "Seems pretty wild to me."

"It's the same all over." Dolman stared down at the pale green vegetation below. "We'll have to go higher. I can't get a bearing this low down."

Doc nodded, his pudgy hands gentle on the controls. Below them the jungle dwindled to a sickly green mass as the machine roared up towards the clouds. "Tell me when."

"I'll tell you." The big man stared down below, trying to fit himself into a familiar pattern in this unfamiliar environment. Then he had stood in the rolling, swaying wreck of a gutted cargo ship, with heat searing his flesh and the screams of the injured in his ears. Ahead of him the Jagged Mountains had loomed high and threatening and he had paid little attention to the falling cargo beneath the streamers of its ribbon parachutes.

"Set down there." He pointed to a spot below. "Anywhere will do for camp." He chuckled as the machine tilted and dropped. "This may be a long job; may as well get comfortable while we can."

Doc nodded, not speaking, his eyes searching for a clearing. He was wasting his time. Before they could land they had to make their own.

The ground was still warm from the napalm bomb when they set up camp. The liquid fire had seared a landing place, burning the undergrowth between the trees and even charring the great giants that soared five hundred feet from the ground. Only charred though; the soggy wood resisted even the chemical fury of napalm. They had ridden the thermal currents as the fire had licked and destroyed the vegetable and insect life below and when the last trace of flame had died they had landed and set up camp.

There were four tents. Shelia had one; Molton had one; the two hard-faced men shared one and Dolman shared with Doc. Each tent contained some stores and supplies and were set in a half circle, the helicopter before them. It was Dolman who insisted on guards.

"There ain't nothing out here that can hurt us," said Sam. He didn't like the idea of watching the jungle with a Dirac over his shoulder.

"You think not?" Dolman was amused. "You've a lot to learn about Venus then. The jungle is full of life, some of it pretty big. A Jumper could wreck the helicopter and ruin the camp. A Rex could wipe us out with a sweep of its tail. Or a Softball could roll up on us."

"What's a Softball?"

"Imagine a man-high sponge covered with whips like barbed wire and you've got a Softball. The barbs are poisoned and the whole thing can move faster than a man can run." Dolman eased the holsters at his waist. He had insisted that everyone be armed with bullet and flame projectors. "Better have one of you circling the camp at all times ready to give warning if you hear something coming." He paused. "Not that you'd hear a Squab."

"A Squab?"

"A thing like a pool of jelly only as big as a football field. It seeps between the trees and folds itself around anything it touches. It can't hurt the trees, of course, but it can tackle anything else."

"You're kidding." Sam looked nervously at the edges of the clearing. .

"I'm not so sure," said Mike suddenly. "I read a book about Venus once."

"Take turns at standing guard," ordered Molton. It ended the argument.

Later, as they sat around the stove drinking coffee, Dolman tried to thaw Shelia's reserve.

"A strange planet, Venus," he said. "Incredibly virile and unbelievably ferocious. The law here is simply kill or be killed, eat or be eaten." He scraped his foot over the black char left by the napalm. Several thin, wire-like shoots were exposed, pale and sickly-looking. "See? Give this place a month and you wouldn't know we'd ever been here."

"Interesting." She was still hostile.

"What I'm trying to point out," Dolman said, "is that we are six people against an alien world. Logic, if nothing else, dictates that we work together for common survival." He smiled at her. "For example, you could be caught by a Whip Vine and I could be the only one around to help. Maybe I wouldn't be too eager to help."

"Are you suggesting that your friendship is for sale?"

"No one can buy friendship, Shelia." Dolman was bitter. "But a man would be a fool to help an enemy. I'm not asking you to love me, just to stop hating me. It would make things a lot easier for the both of us."

"I see." She frowned down at her boots. She, like them all, was wearing Hotland gear, thick boots reaching to the knee, tough breeches and blouse which left only the hands and head bare. The gear was hot and uncomfortable, but it provided protection against the insects and vegetation. In the jungle itself they would wear heavy gloves and a transparent head cover.

"Not that you've any reason to hate me," continued the big man. "I've never done you any harm. In fact I've never even seen you before." He smiled at her, his craggy face becoming suddenly boyish. He held out his hand. "Friends?"

"I . . ." She hesitated, making no attempt to take his hand, then sprang to her feet as Sam, on guard, yelled a hoarse warning. Dolman, moving with incredible speed, knocked up the barrel of the Dirac as it blasted a searing tongue of heat.

"Hold it!"

"But…"

"Hold it!" Dolman stared into the undergrowth and Shelia, at his side, stifled a sudden cry. Something moved towards them.

It was a man, but a man so altered that it was hard to credit him with feeling or intelligence. He stood staring at them, swaying a little, his mouth working and saliva trickling down his chin. He shambled forward, the rents in his rotting clothing revealing ugly sores and festering wounds. Two Hotlanders accompanied him, their scaled hides glistening from condensed moisture.

"Howdy," said the man. He blinked and sniffed the air. "Got a little coffee to spare?" His words were slurred and thick as if he hadn't spoken for a long time. His eyes were red and sore and fever-bright. His hair and beard were matted and covered with filth. Dolman, standing beside Shelia, felt her grip his arm.

"Who is he?" she whispered. "What is he doing here?"

"He's a Zwart hunter." Dolman stared about him and jerked his thumb towards the stove. The hunter and his companions headed for the coffee pot, squatted down and helped themselves to the hot, sweet brew.

"Zwart?" Shelia was puzzled.

"That's right." Dolman hadn't taken his eyes from the trio. "Zwart is a drug. Usually it's collected by the Hotlanders and traded in at Venusburg or Aphrodite. There are a few trading posts scattered through the jungle, but not many. Sometimes an Earthman gets the bright idea of turning collector himself. When he does he usually finishes like our friend there." He moved towards the trio, Shelia following him.

The hunter gulped the last of his brew and stared at the big man. "You got a smoke?"

"Help yourself." Dolman produced a package of cigarettes and threw them towards the man. He caught them, opened them, tossedeach of the Hollanders a couple of the little white cylinders. They grunted, thrust them into their mouths and chewed with obvious satisfaction.

"Name's Murphy," said the hunter. He seemed to think he should identify himself. "You got anything you don't want? Coffee, tobacco, sugar?" He licked his lips. "I can trade."

"Trade what?" Mol ton was interested. He squatted down, well away from the verminous hunter. Sam was back on guard and Doc had insisted that Mike help him with the helicopter. The group around the stove were isolated from the others.

"I got some Zwart." Murphy fumbled in a skin pouch hanging from his belt. He produced a half dozen pods, each about two inches long and of a peculiar liver-grey colour. His cracked and filthy thumbnail pressed against the pods. "Good and ripe and worth plenty at the settlements. You want to trade?"

"What you asking?"

"Anything you've got spare. Tobacco for the boys, coffee, sugar, anything." Murphy's voice trailed into silence as he stared down at. the pods in his hand. He began to tremble, the saliva from his mouth running thicker over his bearded chin. Suddenly, as if yielding to an overpowering command, he thrust one of the pods into his mouth, chewed busily for a few moments, then relaxed.

"Seems as if you need them more than we do," said Dolman. "How long you been out?"

"How long?" Murphy shrugged. "No idea. I lost count a long time ago." His words now were clear, sharp and decisive. "Not that it matters. I've got the Zwart trade well tied up in this area. Another couple of months and I'll be able to retire and take things easy." He lobked at the pods still in his hand and thrust them back into his pouch. "You'll let me have some supplies?"

"I'll see what I can do," promised Dolman. He rose and walked to his tent, leaving Molton talking to the hunter. When he came out Shelia was waiting for him.

"You're not going to give that horrible man anything, are you?"

"Some coffee, tobacco and sugar." Dolman hefted the bundle in his hand. "That's what he asked for and that's what he'll get."

"But why? Why give him anything at all?" She made an expression of disgust. "How could a man sink so low?"

"Zwart." Dolman shrugged at her expression. "It's a habit forming drug," he explained. "On Earth it's used to create a total pain-block for operations. It divorces the mind from contact with reality and permits the patient to dream without awareness of physical pain. That," he said grimly, "is when it is used for medical purposes. Unfortunately, too many people are willing to pay big money for the stuff for private use. Like morphine and cocaine in the old days."

"I understand," she said. "But Murphy?"

"He took to collecting. The Hotlands are no place for Earthmen and so he tried the drug to ease his pain. Then he tried more and so caught the habit. Now he can't live without it, even though it's killing him."

"He looks horrible," she said.

"He eats the raw pods. The outer skin is toxic, but he's beyond worrying about that. He's got to take something to forget the pain of his sores and, anyway, the craving for Zwart is something he can't resist." Dolman hefted the package in his hand. "He'll die, of course, they all do."

"And the Hotlanders? Why do they travel with him?"

"They're keeping him alive," said Dolman. "Without them he wouldn't last a day. They know that he can't last long and are willing to serve him until the end. In return he teaches them Terran so that they can get jobs in the settlements. The final part of their pay comes when he dies." He nodded at her horrified expression. "That's right, the Hotlanders are descended from scavengers."

He left her looking pale and ill.

* * * *

The rotors of the helicopter made a monotonous drone as the machine drifted slowly over the jungle below. Dolman, sitting next to Doc, lifted tired eyes from the radiation detector he carried in his lap and stared at the endless greenery below.

"Getting tired?" The fat man adjusted his controls and glanced at the big man. "Coffee and sandwiches are in the box if you want them."

"Thanks." Dolman rested the detector on the floor and reached behind him. He bit into a sandwich, not tasting the vitamin paste and percholra flour, then took a long drink of coffee. "You want to eat?"

"Later." Doc glanced at the compass. "I want to keep my weight down."

"What for?" Dolman had grown to like the fat, wheezing pilot and on the long trips the liking had increased. Doc, in his own way, was a philosopher. He made no secret of his liking for easy money and Dolman guessed that, if he had to, he could be utterly ruthless.

He sat back, studying the fat man, gauging him and fitting him into the general pattern. Sam and Mike had been easy to fit. They were trigger men, bodyguards, men with unswerving loyalty to Molton. They were not unintelligent, but on Venus they were out of their environment. They belonged to the big cities of Earth. Molton was more of an enigma. He was intelligent, suave and yet determined. Dolman had found proof of that.

The hunter and his two Hotlanders had left the camp when Doc and the big man had returned from their first trip. Molton had said that they had wandered off and there was no reason to doubt his word. But Dolman had taken a walk into the jungle and, trail-wise, had found the hunter. He and the Hotlanders were dead, shot in the back and left to rot. Who had pulled the trigger didn't matter. Molton had given the orders.

It was logical, Dolman supposed. Molton wouldn't want anyone to know where he had been and what he was up to, and yet the slaughter had sickened the big man. It had been unnecessary. Murphy would have died long before reaching civilization. He had said nothing to anyone but, since then, had slept with a loaded gun in his hand and had been careful to guard his back.

"Just about reached the limit of this segment," said Doc. He glanced at Dolman. "It means shifting camp to another site when we get back and starting all over. Molton won't like that."

"Then he'll have to do the other thing." Dolman wasn't worried about the wizened man. Fuel for the helicopter was no problem; the small atomic pile took care of that. Night was something else. With a rotation of thirty days a fifteen day "night" was something to be avoided.

"Are you sure that the cargo is in this area?" Doc turned from his instruments. "Maybe we're just wasting time?"

"I'm not sure of anything." Dolman glanced at the detector. "I think that it landed around here but the last time I saw it was a year ago." He sucked in his breath as a needle kicked on a dial and a signal lamp flashed. "Got something!"

"Where?" Doc adjusted his controls. "Which way?"

"To the right. Hold it!" Dolman swore as the lamp faded. "Too far. Go back and drop lower."

"Can't go too low." Doc swung the machine, the rotors slowing as he cut speed. "Tell me when and I'll drop a marker." Dolman nodded, eyes on the flickering needles of the detector. They jumped, jumped again and held steady as the signal lamp burned brighter. He gave the order at maximum intensity. "Now!"

An object plummeted from the belly of the machine to explode in a billowing cloud of fluorescent orange powder. It was radioactive and luminous in the dark. The needles of the detector jumped to a new high as the powder settled on the trees.

"Nice work," said Doc and eased his cramped back. "Now we can go back and…" He swore as a flock of tug-birds disturbed by the marker suddenly erupted from the jungle below. Scared, vicious, the huge reptiles flapped leathery wings and headed towards what they took to be an enemy.

"The rotors!" Doc fed power to the blades as a wide-jawed reptile dashed itself to death against the cabin. "Dolman! The rotors!"

Dolman tore at the cabin door as the machine fought for altitude. He jerked it open, hanging onto a strut with one hand while he hung outside. The slipstream from the rotors hammered at his exposed head and body but the flame gun in his hand was steady as he squeezed the trigger. Fire spat from the orifice and a tug-bird dissolved into smoking ruin. Again he fired, again, fighting a losing battle with the savage reptiles as they flung themselves towards the spinning vanes. One struck and the machine shuddered as the broken body went spinning down to the jungle below. Immediately the helicopter began to lose altitude.

Despite the broken vane Doc managed to retain control. Dolman fired at the last of the attacking birds and then pulled himself back into the cabin. Doc, his face tense with strain, jerked his head upwards.

"Rotor smashed," he wheezed. "The balance has been lost and the vanes will tear themselves apart."

"Can we get back to the camp before they go?"

"I doubt it." Doc listened to the harsh grating from above. "They may fold at any moment. Best thing I can do is to drop so that when they do go we'll stand a chance." Wheezing, he crouched over the controls.

They crashed five miles from camp, tearing into the vegetation as the rotors folded with a scream of metal, bouncing and crashing as they tumbled through the branches to the ground below. Dolman, aside from bruises, was unhurt, but Doc had stove in a couple of ribs and could taste blood from a torn lung. Dolman strapped him up, wrapping elasta bandage around the fat-covered torso and, carrying what equipment they could, they struck out towards the clearing.

It wasn't an easy journey. Twice the thunder of Dolman's flame gun saved them from an unpleasant death and a dozen times only his knowledge of local conditions enabled them to avoid dangers. The distance was only five miles, but it took nine hours to reach the clearing, and by the time they arrived Doc was spitting blood and Dolman was exhausted from the strain of helping the injured man along.

Molton didn't make things easier.

"So you've lost the helicopter," he said. "I should have known better than to trust it to a fat fool and a drunken bum!"

"Go easy on your words," said Dolman. He felt too tired to argue. "If it's any consolation we found the cargo."

"Where?" Molton was eager.

"About twelve miles due West. We dropped a marker." Dolman smiled at Shelia as she brought him coffee. "We can go after it just as soon as you radio for another helicopter."

"That's out," said Molton flatly. He lowered his voice. "You can see why, can't you? A pilot will have to deliver the machine. He may talk."

"Then send for two machines, one for us and the other to take the pilot back." Dolman sipped at the coffee. "Simple."

"Not so simple. They may see the marker and in any case they may talk." Molton gnawed at his lips. "We'll go collect it ourselves."

"On foot?" Dolman lost some of his weariness. "You're crazy! How do you expect to march through twelve miles of Hotland with a woman and a sick man?" He shook his head. "Count me out if that's on your mind."

"There is an alternative," said Molton softly. "Doc isn't much use to us now. He could stay behind and, if anything should happen to him, then the more for those who are left."

"A quarter million will do me," said Dolman tightly.

"You won't get a cent unless we reach that cargo."

"A threat, Molton?" Dolman dropped his cup, his hand falling to his belt. Molton saw the gesture.

"I don't threaten," he said softly. "And I'd advise you to keep your hand away from your guns. Sam and Mike are watching and they know what to do." He smiled with an artificial friendliness. "You're tired, Dolman, and maybe you can't think straight. We've come too far and are too close to quarrel now."

"Sure," said Dolman. The wizened man was right. He needed sleep before he could think this one out.

"We'll start as soon as you've rested," said Molton. "We'll make a quick march, get what we came for and then head back here. We can radio for a helicopter then."

"All right." Dolman let himself be persuaded. "But Doc comes with us."

But when he awoke the pilot was dead.

* * * *

The march was a nightmare. The Hotlands were un-equalled in the entire System for sheer ferocity and every step was a gamble with .death. Whip Vines lashed at them, their thin, saw-edged tendrils raking the plastic of their clothing. Insects droned about their head covers and the almost invis-ible webs of giant spiders waited to snare them in stickiness. Shelia, stumbling along beside Dolman, asked the question which had been troubling her.

"I can't understand how you managed to survive," she said. "After the *Evening Star* crashed, I mean. I wouldn't have thought that anyone could last a day."

"I was lucky." The big man led the way around what seemed to be a boulder but was a disguised, clam-like thing which could amputate an arm or leg. "We crashed higher on the Jagged Mountains. I must have wandered into the Hot-lands from a safer region. Also they said that I had a couple of natives with me."

"Those scaly things?"

"That's right. They manage to get on pretty well in the jungles. They aren't as dumb as most people think them to be and they have a queer sense of ethics. They'll help a Ter-restrial for the sake of a reward or for the chance of learning the language."

"But you said…" Shelia swallowed, not able to finish the sentence.

"That's their insurance." Dolman wasn't being cynical. "They'll help while they can and, if the Terrestrial should die, then they eat." He gave a short laugh. "Fair enough when you come to think about it. After all, the Terrestrial doesn't object." He turned to where Molton, guarded by Sam and Mike, followed the path he had made. "Let's camp and rest. We've still a long way to go."

They rested and brewed coffee, sitting in the smoke of the smudge-fire to drive away the venomous insects. They slept a little, briefly and in turn, then they resumed the march. They reached the marker twenty-two hours after leaving the original camp.

"It's around here somewhere." Dolman frowned at the dials of the detector he had brought with him. "The marker has a different radiation pattern so we should be able to spot the cargo container pretty easily." He looked at Molton. "Incidentally, now that we're so near, how about telling me just what's so valuable about it?"

"Don't you know?" Molton stared at the big man, a peculiar expression in his eyes.

"I can guess but I could be guessing wrong."

"What you don't know can't hurt you." Molton glanced around. Sam was talking to Shelia as she crouched over a fire. Mike, standing a short distance from the big man, held his Dirac with practised ease. "Let's just say that the cargo container holds something of tremendous value on Earth. If we can obtain it, then we cash in." He shrugged as if annoyed at the waste of time. "We'd be more profitably employed in finding it than talking about it. Let's get to work."

They found it after a ten hour search. Dolman stared at the huge container, still wreathed with the ribbons of its parachute and now overgrown with the sickly green vegetation. Molton made a low noise in his throat as he saw the humped bulk and his eyes, as he glanced at the big man, were glowing with triumph.

"It's it! We've found it!"

"Yes." Dolman stepped towards the container and, with a shot from his flame gun, burned one side free of vegetation. His lips thinned as he stared at the stencilled markings. Molton brushed past him, his gun spouting flame as he seated the door seals into molten ruin. Mike joined him as he tugged open the portal and the two men vanished inside. They came out carrying a sealed container between them, then halted as they saw Dolman.

"All right," he said grimly. "The farce is over. Just drop that thing and raise your hands." The bullet projector in his hand emphasized his words.

"Farce?" Molton raised his eyebrows. "I'm not sure that I know what you're talking about."

"I think you do. I think that that container contains the reason for the sabotage of the *Evening Star.*" Rage thickened the big man's voice. "When I think of what happened to the men in that ship…" He forced himself to be calm. "In any case I'm arresting you for the murder of Murphy and his Hollanders. If that isn't enough, I'm also arresting you for the murder of Doc." His voice thickened again. "If you try to escape it won't bother me in the slightest. I'd be just as happy shooting you as taking you in."

"Indeed?" Molton licked his lips. His eyes flickered to a point over Dolman's shoulder. "So you're going to shoot us, are you?"

"I…." Dolman jerked as he heard the scream, then, as he turned, something smashed against his skull and filled his vision with stars.

* * * *

It was dark and someone, somewhere, was sobbing. It was a peculiar sound, almost familiar, and it held a note of hopeless pleading.

"Dolman. Oh, Dolman! Wake up, Dolman. Wake up."

It was Shelia. Dolman sat upright, groaned at the pain in his head and gritted his teeth as he explored his scalp. A bullet had cut a furrow over his right ear and the blood had dried on his hair and the side of his face. The pain caused by his probing washed away the last of his numbness.

"Dolman!" Shelia was beside him, a warm shape in the darkness. Abruptly she began to cry. "I thought you were dying. I thought I was all alone in this horrible place. I…"

"Shut up!" He was deliberately curt. If he could have seen her he would have slapped her face. His tone did the trick and she lost her hysteria. "I can't see," he said. "Am I blind?"

"No." Her relief at his recovery matched his own. "It's night and it's been dark for a long time."

"Where are we?"

"In the cargo container. I dragged you in here when I found you were still breathing."

"Did you shut the door?" Dolman didn't wait for her answer; he was already groping towards the panel. Metal grated as he tugged at it and light, the pale orange luminescence from the radioactive marker, seeped through the door. It was weak, little more than a dim glow, but to eyes accustomed to utter blackness it served. Cautiously, the big man stepped from the container, found a pool of condensed water and laved his head and torso. He wasn't surprised to find that he was naked but for a pair of pants. He had boots but no guns.

The wash had restored his appetite and he felt ravenous hunger. Still acting with the utmost caution he found and picked an armful of fruits. He handed one to the girl as he stepped back into the container.

"You'd better eat," he ordered. "Tear off the skin and swallow the pulp. You may not like the taste, but eat it just the same." He ripped the tough skin off a fruit with his teeth and filled his mouth with the sour, metallic-tasting pulp.

In the soft light filtering through the door he watched her eat. She, too, had lost her protective clothing and seemed small and helpless in her shorts and halter. Her hair was a mess and her face was dirty. She looked up from the fruit she was eating, conscious of his stare.

"What happened?"

"Sam shot you. I screamed, but it was too late. At first Molton thought you were dead, and when he found you weren't he stripped you and left you where you had fallen."

"I see." Molton knew his business. A helpless man in the Hotlands would be stung and eaten by the swarms of scavengers within a few hours. Shelia, by dragging him into the cargo container, had saved his life. He selected another fruit. "And you?"

"I'd heard what you said and I wanted to know what it was all about." Shelia hesitated. "Molton had told me that you had caused my brother's death and that this trip would obtain evidence against you. That's why I financed the trip."

"Wait a minute!" Dolman stared at her. "Your brother?"

"Yes. My real name is Browley, Shelia Browley. My brother…"

"Was second officer on the *Evening Star.*" Dolman nodded. "And you thought that I'd sabotaged the ship and caused his death, is that it?"

"Yes. Molton told me that he had been working on the case as an undercover man for the S.S. He said that he could prove you were a criminal. I agreed to finance the trip."

"Didn't it ever occur to you that if Molton was telling the truth he wouldn't have needed private backing?"

"He explained that. He said that he'd been refused funds and that the case was closed." She made a helpless gesture. "I was a fool, I suppose, but I wanted to avenge Jack for what had been done to him."

"And then?"

"Then Molton laughed at me when I protested at leaving you here. He said that perhaps you'd like company so he took away my protective clothing, tied me up and dumped me beside you." She held out her hands; her wrists were marked with angry weals. "It was horrible. I kept having to shout and twist to frighten away insects. In the end I managed to free myself and drag you into the container. I shut the door and then I must have fainted or something. When I awoke it was dark and I thought that you were dying."

"Were you stung at all?"

"Yes, at least I think so."

That accounts for it. The venom tends to paralyse. You must have had enough to knock you out and keep you out for several days. Me, too." He sucked at his teeth. "You know, if you hadn't got us inside and shut the door, we wouldn't be alive now."

"It doesn't seem to make any difference." Shelia sat forlornly on a bale of goods. "We're stranded in the Hotlands, without guns or clothing. How can we ever get back to Venusburg?"

Put that way it seemed hopeless.

* * * *

The Hollanders came at dawn, three of them, their scaled bodies glistening in the pearly light. Dolman grinned at them then turned to Shelia.

"Well, what did I tell you?"

"You win," she smiled. She had lost her harried expression and the poisons had left her blood. During the long night they had slept and eaten, slept and eaten, both aching with fever and both fighting the numbness caused by the insect venom. Shortly before dawn Dolman had lit a fire, covering it with soggy leaves and filling the area with smoke. The Hotlanders, as he had guessed, had come to see what they could find.

"They will carry us," said Dolman. He had spoken to the natives, his tongue clicking in their speech, using Terran when his knowledge of their language failed him. He, had used signs and promises and they had understood. "They can make better time that way and will protect us from the jungles."

"How long will it take us to reach Venusburg?"

"We aren't going to Venusburg." Dolman was grim. "We're going to find Molton." He ended the conversation by mounting on the broad back of the largest native.

It wasn't an easy ride. The sinuous reptiles moved in a peculiar gait, their strong back legs eating distance, their heads and forelegs lifted and balanced by their thick tails. The Terrestrials clung to a rope of twisted vines wrapping their legs around the scaled bodies and hanging on as the Hotlanders raced through the soaring trees.

At times they rested, foraging among the undergrowth for succulent dainties, crunching wide-winged insects, multi-legged spiders and the half-animal, half-vegetable crawl-worms which lay in wait to bore their way into the bodies of their prey. The Terrestrials ate nothing but fruit.

During these times of rest Dolman told the girl about himself.

"The trial was a farce," he explained. "The *Evening Star* was sabotaged, a time bomb in the reactor room. We had our suspicions as to who was to blame but no proof. The cargo was the thing; someone was smuggling narcotics to Earth. There's been a lot of trouble caused by that, and the wreck showed just how strong the ring was getting."

"But they blamed you, kicked you out of the S.S." Shelia looked baffled.

"It was rigged." Dolman looked grim. "It was my suggestion and, because it seemed the only way, the S.S. agreed to give it a try. We had no proof," he explained, "only suspicions. Sooner or later the person responsible for the sabotage would try to get his hands on that cargo. So I waited for him to show up."

"You were bait," said Shelia slowly. "Is that it?"

"The cargo was the bait," corrected Dolman. "But I was the only one who knew where it could be found. You see, the ring was well-organized. My guess is that the time bomb was touched off by a radio signal. Someone didn't want that cargo to reach Earth, maybe because the heat was on, and they wanted to remain in the clear. Well, a year has passed and they must have thought it time to act. Molton contacted me, I agreed to lead him to the cargo, the rest you know."

"But where did I come in?" Shelia was puzzled. Dolman explained.

"You provided the perfect cover. Molton, up to the time he left us, was innocent; no court would have convicted him. That's why I had to show my hand. He'd murdered Murphy and Doc, he had what he'd come for; it was only a matter of time before he got rid of us." He shrugged. "I was careless."

"But it'll be all right, won't it?" Shelia glanced around where they sat. Above their heads the great trees soared like the pillars of a cathedral, the soft light from the shielded sun filtering down through the branches, the incessant condensation forming little pools in the leaves and dripping down with the fragile sound of fairy bells. It looked peaceful, harmless, but then a writhing thing with fanged jaws boiled from the ground to die beneath the heel of one of the Hotlanders.

"You'll be able to make charges when we reach Venusburg," she said. "Molton will be caught with the evidence." She looked thoughtful. "Drugs, I suppose?"

"Zwart." Dolman dug his heel into the ground. "Unless we find Molton we won't be seeing Venusburg," he said softly. "We need his radio to signal for a helicopter. Without it we'll die in the jungles." The tinkling fairy-bells seemed to have suddenly gained a new menace.

*   *   *   *

The journey was a nightmare. Without the natives they would not have lasted past their first sleep, and even with the Hotlanders to stand guard their lives were measured. Shelia nursed a swollen leg; an insect had stung it and its venom filled her blood with fire. Dolman, his torso scratched and torn, despite the crude covering of leaves he wore, studied the girl with anxious eyes as they rode their peculiar mounts.

"Bad?"

"I'll manage." Incredibly she managed to smile. "How long?"

"Until we catch up with Molton?" The big man shook his head. "I don't know. I'm relying on the natives to find his trail." He looked at the girl with mounting concern. She was ill, burning with fever and hardly able to sit her mount. Beneath her leaf-cloak her skin was flushed, mottled with angry sores and scarlet pustules. Dolman himself was little better, but as yet he had avoided the worst insects. He leaned forward and hissed at the Hotlander. Speed, now, was more important than ever.

Shelia swayed as the native raced along beneath her. Part of her mind had somehow returned to Earth so that she smelt the warm scents of flowers and felt cool breezes on her skin. The jolting body which sent stabs of pain through her swollen leg seemed to belong to a dream, a nightmare from which she would soon waken. Gripped in fevered delirium she clung to the scaly body while around her the great trees, the poisonous undergrowth and the multitude of winged and clawed insects turned and spun in ever-increasing revolutions.

She opened her eyes and looked up into the anxious face of the big man.

"Better?"

"Should I be?" Cautiously she sat upright. There was a peculiar taste in her mouth, almost as if it had been filled with dust. She swallowed and stood up, a part of her wondering why her swollen leg now gave her no pain.

"Zwart," said Dolman. He held a couple of the liver-coloured pods in his hand. "I had to do something to ease your pain. You were screaming and twisting so much that we had to stop."

"I'm all right," said Shelia. She chuckled, her head clear, her body divorced from pain. She laughed and sang a snatch of a popular song. She felt as if she could run for miles, perform feats of incredible strength or walk unaided to Venusburg. The jungle had lost its terror. She looked at Dolman, feeling the blood rush hot and compelling through her body, filling her with the desire to love and be loved.

"Steady," Dolman hissed to the native. "Mount now and let's get going."

"What's the hurry?" She smiled at him, reaching up and letting her fingers caress his craggy features.

"You'll feel different later on," he promised grimly. "When the drug wears olf you'll wish you were dead and you'll be begging me to give you another pod. The curse of it is that, unless we find Molton soon, I'll have to give it to you. It's the only thing which will keep you going." He swung a leg over the broad back of the native. "Let's make time now; we haven't got as much as I'd like."

Shelia nodded, quite happy to do anything he asked. As they rode she kept her eyes on his broad shoulders. Dolman was all man, a man any woman would be proud of. At first she had hated him; no, hated the thought of what he had done. But she didn't hate him now. She just wanted to be near him for always.

"You're in love," she said to herself. "In love for the first time in your life, and it isn't the drug that makes you think this way. Maybe the drug lets you admit it, but that's all."

Beneath her the Hotlander jerked to a sudden halt. Dolman lifted his arm and sat, listening. The third native who had scouted ahead joined him, the hiss of his language sounding like the echoes from a pit of snakes.

"What's wrong?" Shelia urged her mount close to the others. "What's he saying?"

"We've found Molton," said Dolman grimly. "And he's in trouble. Listen."

From somewhere ahead the sharp reports of gunfire drifted among the trees.

* * * *

They found Molton almost insane with fear as he crouched against a tree firing at a grey, amorphous mass which surged before him. It was a Squab and the giant, jelly-like mass surged and rippled with primitive life. The charred edges opposite Molton writhed and recoiled beneath the fury of the flame-gun. Two fading shadows deep within the great bulk gave mute testimony as to what had happened to Sam and Mike.

"We've got to save him." Dolman slipped from the Hotlander and snatched at a fallen limb. "He's got the radio and without it we're stuck."

"But how?" Shelia, still under the influence of Zwart, looked on the entire situation as a joke. "Let's leave him to be eaten. The radio is plastic, we can pick it up after. Or will that thing eat it, too?"

"Its internal acids will ruin it." Dolman prodded at the mass before him. "If we can manage to turn it…"

With a bigger Squab it would have been impossible, but this one was relatively small. Again and again Dolman lashed at the creeping mass, exciting it, tempting it with the nearness of edible food, showering it with blood from his own body. Slowly the thing ebbed away from Molton, reaching blindly for the appetising flesh it could sense so near. Then, when it had started to move, Dolman urged the Hollanders to race from before it and around its edge. Molton, still dazed with fear, still pulling the trigger of his exhausted weapon, was quickly overpowered and bound.

Later, when a smudge-fire had been lit and Dolman enjoyed the sweet taste of coffee, he recovered a little.

"You're a fool, Dolman. That Zwart is worth all of three million on Earth. A third of it could be yours."

"How long would I live to enjoy it?" Dolman glanced to where Shelia rested in uneasy slumber. The Hotlanders squatted somewhere out of sight, enjoying the tobacco and coffee the big man had given them. "You tried to kill me once, remember."

"That was business." Molton licked nervously at his lips. "What else could I do once I'd learned that you were working for the S.S.? Killing you was sheer self-defence."

"Your defence wasn't good enough. I'm still arresting you for murder, sabotage and smuggling." Dolman looked grim. "Just to ease your mind, I'm an accredited officer of the S.S. The arrest is legal. And so would my killing you be if you try to escape."

"Escape." Sweat beaded Molton's forehead as he glanced at the radio. The signal had been sent and even now a helicopter would be on its way. It would home in on the signal, hover, lower a rope ladder and take them all back to civilization.

"Listen," he gasped. "A million clear if you get me back with the stuff and forget the charges." He sounded desperate. "You know what they'll do to me if they get me. Hypnotic probes, the works. They'll open my brain and find out everything."

"That," said Dolman easily, "is the general idea."

"A million and a half!" Molton strained at his bonds. "Don't be a fool, Dolman, what have you to lose? Do you want to spend the rest of your life riding the cans?"

"This may surprise you," said Dolman tightly, "but the answer is yes. I like money, but I'd like to see you and your kind burn even more. I'm thinking of the men who died in the *Evening Star.* I'm thinking of all the rackets you and your kind have smeared over space. You won't understand this, Molton, but some things are worth more than money."

"I said that you were a fool. Now you're proving it."

"Maybe. But I'm in the clear while you're on the way out, smart guy." The flush in Molton's cheeks showed that the sarcasm had registered.

Abruptly Dolman was sick of the whole mess. He was tired of playing a part, of living in filth and risking his life for the sake of an ideal. He wanted to be back in uniform again, riding the spaceships between the planets with the clear, cold, distant beauty of the stars all around him.

With Shelia, he hoped, by his side.

www.ingramcontent.com/pod-product-compliance
Lightning Source LLC
Chambersburg PA
CBHW020145180626
46810CB00004B/1745